Should He Follow Her?

How could he not follow her after such a clear indication of interest?

Matthew waded through the dancers as politely as he could, chasing after the only thing he could recall being interested in for eighteen very long, very cold months.

When he paused under a grand arch between the two rooms, he saw her. He had the distinct impression she felt just as he did.

Though maybe she'd been flirting and it hadn't meant anything.

He cursed under his breath. It had been far too long since he'd dated to remember the rules, which was saying something for a guy who thrived on rules. But this was Venice, not Dallas, and he could be someone else.

There were no rules.

They locked gazes across the room and he went after her.

* * *

Dear Reader,

In *Marriage with Benefits,* Lucas, the hero, had an older brother. Matthew Wheeler was supposed to be a minor secondary character who inspired Lucas to become a man worthy of Cia. The idea of Matthew fading into the background went out the window almost immediately! He came alive on the page and boy, did he ever have a story—the death of his wife broke him. The only solution to stop his pain was to leave everything he'd ever known and set off in search of a way to restart his life.

I've received a *lot* of mail from readers asking what happened to Matthew after the close of *Marriage with Benefits.* I'm so thrilled by your interest because I loved writing about his journey back to the land of the living courtesy of Evangeline LaFleur, a former pop star with scars of her own. A chance meeting one magical night in Venice opens the door to a new future...if only they can overcome the deep-set hooks of the past. This is a tale of two people discovering who they truly are and embracing what is instead of mourning what once was.

It took a while to get Matthew and Evangeline's story to you, but I hope you'll find it was worth the wait.

I love to hear from readers. Visit me online at www.katcantrell.com.

Kat

PREGNANT BY MORNING

—

KAT CANTRELL

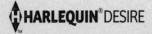
HARLEQUIN® DESIRE

Recycling programs
for this product may
not exist in your area.

ISBN-13: 978-0-373-73291-3

PREGNANT BY MORNING

Copyright © 2014 by Katrina Williams

This edition published by arrangement with Harlequin Books S.A.

For questions and comments about the quality of this book, please contact us at CustomerService@Harlequin.com.

Printed in U.S.A.

Books by Kat Cantrell

Harlequin Desire

Marriage with Benefits #2212
The Things She Says #2218
The Baby Deal #2247
Pregnant by Morning #2278

Other titles by this author available in ebook format.

KAT CANTRELL

read her first Harlequin novel in third grade and has been scribbling in notebooks since she learned to spell. What else would she write but romance? She majored in literature, officially with the intent to teach, but somehow ended up buried in middle management at Corporate America, until she became a stay-at-home mom and full-time writer.

Kat, her husband and their two boys live in north Texas. When she's not writing about characters on the journey to happily-ever-after, she can be found at a soccer game, watching the TV show *Friends* or listening to '80s music.

Kat was the 2011 Harlequin So You Think You Can Write winner and a 2012 RWA Golden Heart finalist for best unpublished series contemporary manuscript.

To my sister. Our trip to Italy remains
one of my most cherished memories.

One

Matthew Wheeler stepped into the fray of Carnevale not to eat, drink or be merry, but to become someone else.

Venice attracted people from all over the globe for its beauty, history or any number of other reasons, but he doubted any of the revelers thronging Piazza San Marco had come for the same reason he had.

Matthew adjusted the tight mask covering the upper half of his face. It was uncomfortable, but necessary. Everyone wore costumes, some clad in tuxedos and simple masks like Matthew, and many in elaborate Marie Antoinette–style dresses and feathered headpieces. Everyone also wore smiles, but that was the one thing he couldn't summon.

"Come, my friend." Vincenzo Mantovani, his next-door-neighbor, clapped Matthew on the shoulder. "We join the party at Caffe Florian."

"*Va bene*," Matthew replied, earning a grin from the Italian who had appointed himself Matthew's Carnevale guide this evening. Vincenzo appointed himself to a lot of things, as long as they were fun, reckless and ill-advised, which made him the appropriate companion for a man who wanted to find all of the above but had no clue how to accomplish it.

Actually, Matthew would be happy if he could just forget about Amber for a few hours, but the ghost of his wife followed him everywhere, even to Italy, thousands of miles from her grave.

Vincenzo chattered in accented English as he and Matthew pushed through the crowd along the edges of Piazza San Marco and squeezed into Caffe Florian, where it was too loud to converse. Which suited Matthew. He had the right companion, but he wasn't sure Vincenzo did.

Like most Venetians, the man had never met a stranger and had immediately latched onto the American living by himself in the big, lonely palazzo next door. Vincenzo's description, not Matthew's, though he couldn't deny it had some truth. He'd outbid an Arab prince by the skin of his teeth to buy the palazzo overlooking the Grand Canal as a wedding gift to Amber, but they'd never made it to Italy in the eleven months after the wedding. He'd been too busy working.

Then it was too late.

Matthew sipped the cappuccino his new friend had magically produced and summoned up a shred of merriment. If he planned to think about something other than Amber, dwelling on her wasn't going to work. She would hate him like this, would want him to move on, and he was trying. His sole goal this evening was to be someone who wasn't grieving, someone who didn't have the weight of responsibility and his family's expectations on his shoulders. Someone who fit into this fantastical, hedonistic Carnevale atmosphere.

It was hard to be someone else when he'd been a Wheeler since birth.

Matthew, along with his brother, father and grandfather, comprised the foundation of Wheeler Family Partners, a multimillion-dollar commercial real estate firm that had been brokering property deals in North Texas for over a century. Matthew had firmly believed in the power of family and tradition, until he lost first his wife, then his grand-father. Grief had so paralyzed him the only solution had been to leave.

He was a runaway from life, pure and simple. He had to find a way to get back to Dallas, back to the man he'd been.

The beaches of Mexico had failed to produce an answer. Machu Picchu had just exhausted him. The names of the other places he'd been had started to blur, and he had to do something different.

A month ago, he'd ended up in Venice. Until real life felt doable again, this was where he'd be.

Near eleven o'clock, Vincenzo herded a hundred of his closest friends—and Matthew—the few blocks to his house for a masked ball. The narrow streets allowed for only a few partygoers to pass simultaneously, so by the time Matthew arrived at the tail end of the group, the palazzo next door to his was already ablaze with lights and people. In marked contrast, Matthew's house was dark.

He turned his back on it and went up the stone steps to Vincenzo's back entrance. The sounds of Carnevale blasted from the palazzo, drowning out the quiet lap of the canal against the water entrance at the front.

Inside, a costumed attendant took his cloak. An ornate antique table in the hall blocked Matthew's path to the main area, an oddity with its large glass bowl in the center full of cell phones.

"It's a phone party."

The gravelly voice came from behind him, and he turned to find the owner.

A woman. Masked, of course, and wearing a delicate embroidered dress in pale blue and white with miles of skirts. The neckline wasn't as low cut as almost every other female's, but in combination with so much dress, her softly mounded breasts drew his eye. Whimsical silver butterfly wings sprouted from her back.

"Was my confusion that obvious?" he asked, his gaze firmly on her face.

She smiled. "You're American."

"Is that the explanation for why I don't know what a phone party is?"

"No, that's because you have more maturity than most of the people here."

So she must know the guests, then. Except for Vincenzo, who had disappeared, Matthew knew no one. This little butterfly was an interesting first encounter.

Most of her face was covered, with the exception of a full mouth painted pink. Caramel-colored hair hung in loose curls around her bare shoulders. Stunning. But her voice...it was sultry and deep, with a strange ragged edge that caught him in the gut.

He'd been looking for a distraction. Perhaps he'd found one.

"Now I'm curious. Care to enlighten me?" he asked.

She shrugged with a tiny lift of her shoulders. "Women drop their phone into the bowl. Men pick one out. Voila. Instant hookup."

His eyebrows rose. Vincenzo partied much differently than Matthew had been expecting. "I honestly have no good response."

"So you won't be fishing one out at the end of the evening?"

A tricky question. The old Matthew would say absolutely not. He'd never had a one-night stand in his life, never even considered it. This kind of thing had his brother, Lucas, written all over it. Lucas might have pulled out two phones and somehow convinced both women they'd been looking for a threesome all along. Well, once upon a time he would have, but in a bizarre turn of events, his brother was happily married now, with a baby on the way.

Matthew did not share his brother's talent when it came to women. He knew how to broker a million-dollar deal for a downtown Dallas high-rise and knew how to navigate the privilege of his social circle but nothing else, especially not how to be a widower at the age of thirty-two.

When Matthew left Dallas, intent on finding a way to move on after Amber's death, he'd had a vague notion of becoming like Lucas had been before marrying his wife, Cia. Lucas always had fun and never worried about consequences. Matthew, like his father and grandfather before him, had willingly carried the weight of duty and family and tradition on his shoulders, eagerly anticipating the day his wife would give birth to the first of a new generation of Wheelers. Only to have it all collapse.

Becoming more like Lucas was better than being Matthew, and nothing else had worked to pull him out of this dead-inside funk. And he had to pull out of it so he could go home and pick up his life again.

So what would Lucas do?

"Depends." Matthew nodded to the bowl. "Is yours in there?"

With a throaty laugh, she shook her head. "Not my style."

Strangely, he was relieved and disappointed at the same time. "Not mine, either. Though I might have made an exception in this one case."

Her smile widened and she drew closer, rustling her wings. The front of her dress brushed his chest as she leaned in to whisper in her odd, smoky voice, "Me, too."

Then she was gone.

He watched her as she swept into the main room of Vincenzo's palazzo and was swallowed by the crush. It was intriguing to be so instantly fascinated by a woman because of her voice. Should he follow her? How could he not follow her after such a clear indication of interest?

Maybe she'd been flirting and it hadn't meant anything. He cursed under his breath. It had been far too long since he'd dated to remember the rules. Actually, he'd never understood the rules, even then, which was saying something for a guy who thrived on rules. But this was Venice, not Dallas, and he was someone else.

There were no rules.

Matthew followed Butterfly Woman into the crowd.

Electronic music clashed with old-world costumes, but no one seemed to notice. Dancers dominated the floor space on the lower level of the palazzo. But none of the women had wings.

Along the edges of the dance floor, partygoers tried their luck at roulette and vingt-et-un, but he didn't bother to look for his mystery woman there. Gambling was for those who knew nothing about odds, logic or common sense, and if she fell into that category, he'd rather find a different distraction.

A flash of silver caught his eye, and he glimpsed the very tips of her wings as she disappeared into another room.

"Excuse me." Matthew waded through the dancers as politely as he could and chased after the only thing he could recall being interested in for eighteen very long, very cold months.

When he paused under a grand arch between the two rooms, he saw her. She stood at the edge of a group of people engrossed in something he couldn't see. And he had the distinct impression she felt as alone in the crowd as he did.

Tarot junkies crowded around Madam Wong as if she held the winning lottery numbers. Evangeline La Fleur was neither a junkie nor one to buy lottery tickets, but people were always amusing. Madam Wong turned over another card and the crowd gasped and murmured. Evangeline rolled her eyes.

Her neck prickled and she sensed someone watching her.

The guy from the hall.

They locked gazes across the room, and she gave herself a half second to let the shiver go all the way down. Delicious. There'd been something about the way he talked to her, as if truly interested in what she had to say. About Vincenzo's stupid phone party, no less.

Lately, no one was interested in what she said, unless it was to answer the question, *"What are you going to do now that you can't sing anymore?"* They might as well ask what she'd do after they nailed the coffin shut.

Hall guy's suit was well-cut, promising what lay underneath it might be worth a peek or two, his lips below the black velvet mask were strong and full and his hands looked…capable. The man trifecta.

The music faded into the background as he strode purposefully toward her without so much as glancing at what he passed. Every bit of his taut focus was on her, and it had a powerful effect, way down low in places usually reserved for men she'd known far longer.

Boldly, she watched him approach, her gaze equally as fixed on him.

Bring it, Tall, Blond and Gorgeous.

The mystery of his masked face somehow made him more attractive. That and the fact he couldn't possibly know who she was behind her mask. This…pull was all about anonymity, and she'd have called anyone a dirty liar who said she'd like it. But she did. When was the last time she'd been within a forty-foot radius of someone who wasn't aware of how her career had crashed and burned? Or the number of Grammys she'd won, for that matter.

For a time, she'd dwelled in the upper echelon of entertainers—so successful she didn't require a last name. The world knew her simply as Eva.

Then she was cast aside, adrift and alone, with no voice.

"There you are," he murmured, as if afraid to be overheard and determined to keep things between them very private. "I'd started to think you'd flown away."

She laughed, surprising herself. Laughter didn't come easily, not lately. "The wings only work after midnight."

"I'd better move fast, then." The eyes on her were beautiful, an almost colorless, crystalline blue that contrasted with the black border of the mask. "My name is—"

"No." She touched a finger to his lips. "No names. Not yet."

As he looked very much like he wanted to suck her fingertip into his mouth, she dropped it before she let him. This stranger was exciting, no doubt, but she had a healthy survival instinct. Vincenzo's friends were a little on the wild side. Even for her.

Yet she'd been following Vincenzo around Europe for a couple of months and couldn't seem to find anything better to do. She wanted to. Oh, how she wanted to. But what?

"Are you seeking your fortune, then?" He nodded to Madam Wong and the crowd parted.

Madam Wong shuffled her cards. "Come. Sit."

Tall, Blond and Gorgeous pulled the brocade chair away from the draped table. Evangeline couldn't see a way to gracefully refuse without drawing unwanted attention, so she sat, extremely aware of the capable hand resting on the back of the chair inches from her neck.

When Madam Wong shoved the deck across the table, Evangeline cut it about a third of the way down and let the fortune-teller restack the cards.

After that quack doctor butchered her vocal cords, Evangeline had spent three months searching for a cure, eventually landing on the doorstep of every Romanian gypsy, every Asian acupuncturist and every Nepalese faith healer she could find.

No one had a way to restore her damaged voice. Or her damaged soul. In short, this wasn't her first tarot reading, and she had little hope it would be any more helpful than all the other mumbo jumbo.

The only positive from the nightmare of the past six months came from winning the lawsuit against the quack doctor, who no longer had a license to practice medicine, thanks to her.

The costumed crowd pressed closer as Madam Wong began laying out the spread. Her brow furrowed. "You have a great conflict, yes?"

Oh, however did you guess? Evangeline waited for the rest of the hokey wisdom.

The withered old woman twirled one of the many rings on her fingers as she contemplated the cards. "You have been cut deeply and lost something precious."

The capable hand of the masked stranger brushed her hair. Evangeline sat up straighter and frowned.

Cut.

She had been, in more ways than one.

"This card…" Madam Wong tapped it. "It confuses me. Are you trying to conceive?"

"A baby?" Evangeline spit out the phrase on a heavy exhale and took another breath to calm her racing pulse. "Not even close."

"Conception comes in many forms and is simply a beginning. It is the step after inspiration. You have been inspired. Now you must go forth and shape something from it."

Inspiration. That was in short supply. Evangeline's throat convulsed unexpectedly. The music in her veins had been abruptly silenced and she hadn't been inspired to write one single note since the surgery from hell.

Madam Wong swept the cards into a pile and began shuffling. "I must do a second spread."

Speechless and frozen, Evangeline tried to shake her head. Her eyes began to burn, a sure sign she'd start bawling uncontrollably very soon. It was the wrong time of the month for this sort of emotional roller coaster.

She needed a code word to get her out of this situation. Her manager had always given her one, so if the press asked a sensitive question, she'd say it and he'd rescue her.

Except she had no manager and no code word. She had nothing. She'd been rejected by everyone—music, the industry, fans. Her father.

"I believe you promised me a dance."

Tall, Blond and Gorgeous clasped her hand and pulled her out of the chair in one graceful move.

"Thank you," he said to Madam Wong, "but we've taken enough of your time. Good evening."

And like that, he whirled her away from the table, away from the prying eyes.

By the time he stopped in an alcove between the main dance floor and the back room, her pulse had slowed. She blinked away the worst of the burn and stared up at her savior. "How did you know?"

He didn't pretend to misunderstand. "You were so tense, the chair was vibrating. I take it you don't care for tarot."

"Not especially. Thanks." After a beat, when it became apparent he wasn't going to ask any questions—which almost made her weep in gratitude—she made a show of scouting around for a nonexistent waiter. "I could go for a glass of champagne. You?"

The thought of alcohol almost made her nauseous, but she needed a minute alone.

"Sure. Unless you'd rather dance?"

"Not right now."

Actually, she was thinking seriously about ditching the party and going to her room. A headache had bloomed behind her eyes. Except her room was right above the dance floor and Vincenzo's other guests had taken the rest of the rooms.

"Be right back. Stay here." Her stranger vanished into the crowd.

Maybe she could quietly gather her things and check into Hotel Danieli, with no one the wiser.… She groaned. As if. She had a better chance of finding solid gold bars on the street than an empty hotel room in Venice during Carnevale.

The stranger returned quickly with two champagne flutes, and she smiled brightly, clinking her rim to his in a false show of bravado. Yes, he was gorgeous and intuitive, but she wasn't going to be good company tonight. She nursed the drink and tried to think of an exit strategy when over his shoulder, she caught sight of her worst nightmare.

It was Rory. With Sara Lear.

Of course he was with Sara Lear. Sara's debut album full of bubblegum pop and saccharine love songs had burned up the charts and was still solidly at number one. The little upstart hadn't worn a mask, preferring to bask in the glow of stardom. Rory was also unmasked, no doubt to make doubly sure everyone knew who was with Sara. He was nothing if not savvy about his own career and his band Reaper made few bones about their desire to headline one of the major summer concert series. Hitching his wagon to a star was an old pattern.

Evangeline had flushed his engagement ring down the toilet after he dumped her and gladly told him to go to hell when he asked for it back.

Rory and Sara strolled through the main room as if they owned it, and why wouldn't they? Both of them had functional vocal cords and long, vital careers ahead of them. Six months ago, Evangeline would have been on Rory Cartman's arm, blissfully in love, blissfully at the top of her career and still blind to the cruelty of a world that loved a success but shunned a has-been.

The headache slammed her again.

She knocked back the champagne in one swallow and tried to figure out how to get past Rory and Sara without being recognized. Sara, she wasn't so worried about; they'd never officially met. But her ex-fiancé would out her in a New York minute without a single qualm. A mask only went so far with someone who knew her intimately.

She couldn't take the questions or the pitying looks or the eyes watching her navigate a very public meeting with the guy who'd shattered her heart and the woman who'd replaced her in his bed. And on the charts.

"More champagne?" her companion asked.

Rory and his new Pop Princess girlfriend stopped a few yards from the shadowy alcove where she stood with the masked stranger. She couldn't step out into the light and couldn't risk standing there with no shield.

Desperate times, desperate measures.

Praying she'd read him right, she plucked the half-empty flute from her savior's hand, set both glasses on the ledge behind her and grasped the lapels of his tux. With a yank, she hauled him into a kiss.

The moment their lips connected, the name Rory Cartman ceased to have any meaning whatsoever.

Two

Matthew had only a moment to register her intent. It wasn't long enough. When the winged woman pressed her lips to his, his body lit up and flooded with heat. She was like a conduit to a nuclear reactor, and the shocking sensation of her warm mouth on his threatened to bring on full meltdown.

He knew precisely what Lucas would do in this situation.

Cupping her face with both palms, Matthew tilted her head to slant his mouth against hers at a deeper angle. Her lips parted on a sigh, and the hands holding his lapels tightened, drawing him closer.

Nearly groaning, he kissed this nameless butterfly until he couldn't think, couldn't stop, almost couldn't stand. The shock of awareness and incendiary carnal lust picked up where his brain failed.

Shocking. And yet familiar. As if they'd done this before, exactly this way, pressed against each other in the shadows. Their lips fit, their bodies slid together with ease. He was kissing a stranger—a nameless stranger—and it should feel wrong, or at least odd.

It was so very right.

This woman was not at all his type—too glittery, too sensual, too beautiful. He couldn't imagine introducing her to his mother or taking her to a museum opening where they'd rub shoulders with the elite of Dallas.

But he didn't care.

For the first time since Amber died, he felt alive. His heart beat in his chest and blood flowed through his veins and a woman was kissing him. He reveled in these small clues that he hadn't been buried alongside his wife.

After an eternity passed in a blink, she broke away and stared up at him, her breath coming in short gasps. "I'm sorry."

"For what?"

He hadn't kissed a woman other than Amber in five years and as a reintroduction to the art, it was off the map. Surely she'd felt some of the same heat.

"I shouldn't have done that," she said.

"Yes, you absolutely should have."

He might be out of practice, but she was still firmly in his arms, and a woman who hadn't just had her world shaken to the foundation would have stepped away by now.

She inhaled sharply, her chest pushing against his and stroking the flame higher. "Not under false pretenses. I have to come clean. My ex is here, and that was a poor attempt to hide from him."

"I beg to differ. As attempts go, I thought it was pretty good."

A quavery laugh slipped out from her kiss-reddened lips and then she did step away, out of his embrace. But not too far.

"Just so you know, I don't go around kissing random men."

"There's an easy way to fix that. I'd be happy to introduce myself and thus eliminate the randomness."

"That would be awesome because I'm pretty sure I'm going to kiss you again."

She *had* felt it.

The thrill swept all the way to the soles of his feet. Tonight, he was someone else, and as it seemed to be working out well so far, why screw around with it?

"Matt. My name is Matt."

It flowed from his mouth effortlessly, though he'd never been Matt in his life. But right here, right now, he liked Matt a hell of lot. Matt wasn't bogged down in inertia and terrified he'd never find his way out. Matt hadn't walked away from all his responsibilities at home or lain awake at night, eaten with guilt over it. Matt hadn't drifted around the world in search of something he suspected didn't exist, only to land in Venice holed up in a cold, lonely palazzo.

Matt had fun and kissed costumed women at parties and maybe got to second base before the end of the night.

She smiled. "Nice to meet you, Matt. You can call me Angie."

Angie. It was too harsh, too common for such a delicate and ethereal woman. The careful phrasing tipped him off that it wasn't her real name, but since he'd similarly hedged, he couldn't exactly complain.

"Which one is your ex? So we can steer clear."

Since she'd been trying to hide, he assumed the breakup had been nasty and not Angie's choice.

Surreptitiously, she glanced behind her, then faced him again. Her soft brown eyes bored into his, luminous with appreciation. "He's over there, on the couch with the little blonde."

Matthew located what had to be the couple she meant. They were locked in a torrid embrace, and the guy's hands were down the blonde's dress. Ouch. Not only was her ex at the same party but also not much for public decency.

"They didn't get the memo? This is a masked ball."

"I like you," she said with a decisive nod.

He grinned. "I like you, too."

"That's good, because I intend to thoroughly use you. I hope you won't be offended."

Matthew's eyebrow shot up. "That depends, I suppose, on what you plan to use me for. And I really hope it's in the same vein as kissing me to hide from lover boy over there."

Apparently Matt knew how to flirt, too. There was no other explanation for such blatant come-ons.

Her tongue wet her lips, and the way she did it—while eyeing his lips at the same time—clamped down hard on his lower half. "You just became my new boyfriend."

"Excellent. I didn't realize I'd applied, but I'm gratified to have survived the rigorous selection process."

She laughed, and that gravelly timbre sliced through his gut anew. "Just for tonight. I can't stand the thought of anyone feeling sorry for me because I'm here alone. Pretend we're together, and I'll buy you breakfast."

Breakfast? He might be in for an evening with a little more action than he'd envisioned.

Was that what he wanted?

"I'm not the slightest bit offended. Unless I'm the backup choice. Is your real boyfriend otherwise engaged?"

"Very nicely done. But unnecessary. You don't have to be all casual-like if you want to know whether I'm available. Just ask."

Dang, he *was* out of practice. But dating had felt like such a betrayal. For so long, he couldn't, and when he finally deemed himself ready, no one appealed to him. Even if he'd dated every one of the sophisticated, demure women in Dallas angling for an invitation to dinner, none of them had wings.

He swallowed and dived in. "Angie, are you seeing anyone?"

"Yeah, this guy named Matt." She stood on tiptoe to whisper in his ear, like she'd done in the hall when they first met. It was becoming something he enjoyed thoroughly. "And he's really hot, too."

"Really?" No one had ever referred to him as hot. At least not to his face. The notion buzzed through his heightened senses and settled in nicely. "I must know more about this guy."

"I'd like to, as well. Vincenzo's got a great balcony on the second floor. Grab a couple of glasses of champagne and meet me there."

She turned and threw a saucy glance over her shoulder as she swayed in the direction of the stone staircase beyond the roulette tables.

He couldn't comply fast enough. Lucas would definitely see what this sexy little butterfly had in mind, and Matt was pretty curious, too. This was one night where anything might happen, and for once, he was looking forward to the possibilities.

The balcony overlooked a closed-off side courtyard that had fallen into disrepair. The small space above was poorly lit and cold, but had the bonus of being Rory and Sara free.

Evangeline was confident Matt wouldn't recognize Rory, as her new friend didn't seem the type to listen to punk rock, but her ex-fiancé's picture did end up next to hers with alarming frequency, even six months later. She couldn't be too careful.

Vincenzo's entertainment system vibrated the stone below her feet. In the distance, the revelry at San Marco drifted along the streets, wrapping the city in festive noise. Singing, instruments, the pop of what might be fireworks, all of it blended into the mystique that was Carnevale. And, for a moment, she was by herself at the world's largest party.

She didn't have to wait long for Matt. Her masked companion came through the unlocked French door with two champagne flutes balanced expertly in one capable hand. It was February in Venice, but the shiver that twisted her back had nothing to do with the temperature.

Thank God she hadn't ditched him. If she had, she'd have

run smack into Rory and missed the single most perfect kiss in the history of time. As stand-in boyfriends went, Matt had it going on. And he'd kissed her headache away, too.

She could find worse company to stave off the perpetual loneliness. Especially among Vincenzo's friends.

Matt handed her a glass and clinked the rims in an echo of their first toast. "This balcony is very difficult to find. How did you know it was here?"

Without the muddle of loud music, his voice was nice—clear, with a hint of the South running through it.

"I'm staying with Vincenzo. My room is down the hall."

"Oh? How do you know Vincenzo, Angie?"

Only her mother called her Angie, so it had seemed safe enough to use the name, though she regretted the necessity. Matt was a genuinely nice human being, someone she'd probably never have connected with under normal circumstances.

"Friend of a friend. You?"

As he was well-spoken and had far more class than Vincenzo's typical wealthy, spoiled buddies, she'd pegged him as a casual acquaintance.

"I'm staying next door."

Well, that made sense. Here on business and renting for the duration, most likely.

"Will you be in Venice long?"

Below the mask, his mouth turned down. "I'm not sure."

As she knew exactly the tone one used to say *back off*, she didn't press him, though now she was curious what his business in Venice might be. Shipping, maybe. She'd never dated a businessman and rarely interacted with people in that realm unless it involved contracts.

Whatever his livelihood, it was to remain a secret for the time being, and since she had secrets of her own, that was fine. She tossed back some champagne, let the bubbles fizz across her tongue and contemplated this very intriguing stand-in boyfriend.

Of course, if they stayed on this balcony, she didn't really need a companion, coerced or otherwise, as a shield from questions and ex-fiancés. So maybe she needed him for something else entirely.

She was alone in the most romantic city in the world, and Matt represented a golden opportunity to change that for one magical evening, then leave before he realized who she was. Loneliness went hand in hand with the fresh scars of rejection that kept reminding her not to let anyone get too close.

But an anonymous encounter—that was a horse of a different color. If he didn't know who she was, he couldn't reject *her*.

The direction of her thoughts heated her up fast despite the chill in the air. But who could blame her for going there when the man's mouth made her blood boil?

There was this strange awareness between them, which she'd felt the moment he'd turned to face her in the foyer. It was almost a recognition, as if she'd seen him many times, but had never quite caught up with him to start a conversation.

Yet he'd never removed his mask. She knew he had a chiseled jaw to match his well-defined mouth and a solid chest under his lapels, but that was it. The rest of his face remained hidden, like his body, his hopes, his disappointments…the mystery of it whet her appetite for more.

"Ever been on a speed date?" she asked him.

He took a sip of champagne and shook his head. "Can't say that I have."

She doubted he'd ever have a need to resort to such a thing. Dating as a whole never worked for her. Men usually fell into three categories: starstruck, unavailable or opportunist.

Rory was firmly in the last category. His rejection had been crushing, especially after losing her voice. She'd thought of all people, he'd understand and would sympathize. That he'd be there for her during the worst crisis of her life. Instead, he couldn't dump her fast enough. On the bright side, he'd cured her of any desire to have a man in her life permanently.

Which made her masked friend exactly what the doctor ordered.

"I haven't either, but I always wanted to. It seems like fun."

"I'm always up for fun. What does it entail?"

She loved the way he talked, like it never occurred to him that normal people's vocabulary didn't usually include words like *entail*. And like it never occurred to him that she hadn't gone to college. He treated her as if she possessed intelligence. That was potent.

"Well, to the best of my knowledge, there's a time limit. We have to get to know each other as quickly as possible before the bell rings. It's designed so you can figure out if you're compatible in a short period of time."

He cocked his head, lips pursed. "I already know I like you. Why do we need to have a speed date to figure that out?"

She shook her head, gaze glued to his. A part of her wanted to take this instant attraction to its natural conclusion as fast as possible. But no smart girl jumped into the pool without at least some clue how deep it was.

"Consider it part of the application process. There's a spark here, and I'm curious to see what happens if we fan it."

His irises flared. "Just so I'm clear, how does the time limit factor in?"

"Ask as many questions as you want, as fast as you can, and when the timer on my phone goes off, you're going to kiss me."

His palm cupped her face, tilting it up to almost meet his. "What if we skip the timer and I kiss you right now?"

"That's no fun." She firmly removed his hand from her chin, only to lose it to her hair as he threaded his fingers through the loose curls not caught up in her feather head-piece.

His warm thumb rested in the hollow behind her ear, brushing it lightly. "Clearly you need a refresher on how good my lips feel on yours."

The shiver went deeper this time, and a nice little hum zipped along her skin, tightening all her erogenous zones into an ache she'd not experienced in a long time. Apparently the speed date was unnecessary to fan the spark.

"Where's your sense of adventure? Five minutes."

She pulled her phone from the clutch tied to a string at her waist and tapped up the timer. She set it on the stone ledge behind Matt, then locked onto the ice-blue of his eyes. Anticipation was one of her favorite parts, and she'd happily drag it out as long as she could.

"I'll go first," he said. "How many times have you seduced a man on a balcony?"

She couldn't help but laugh. Was that what she was doing? "Never. I'm making all sorts of exceptions for you."

"How many times have you seduced a man period?"

"Once or twice. I'm not one to apologize for having a healthy sex drive. Should I?"

"Not to me. Maybe to all the other men down there who are missing out. Your turn."

"I'm naked. What do you do first?"

"Fall down on my knees and weep with joy. Did you really mean to ask what I'd do second?"

Oh, yeah, she really did like Matt. There was something to be said for a guy who could make her laugh with such regularity. "That is what I meant, and before you get all smart-alecky with me, go ahead and hit me with third, fourth and fifth."

"Did I buy you dinner first?"

"Who cares? I'm naked or did you forget?"

"Oh, no, my gorgeous little butterfly, I did not forget. I

asked because I'm trying to get a solid picture in my head of the scene."

His hand pressed on her nape, oh-so-slightly, and her head fell back. His lips grazed the corner of her mouth, not quite touching, but close enough to send a frisson of sparkling heat all the way down to her core.

Well, she hadn't intended for this speed date to descend into foreplay, but okay. It was *sizzling*. And personal information, like their secret professions, or lack thereof in her case, wasn't likely to come up.

"Are you naked on a bed after I've undressed you?" he murmured against her jaw, breath fanning the uncovered part her of face and making her ache to turn into those lips to complete the connection. "Or naked in the shower and have no idea I'm about to join you? Naked, but asleep and I'm going to awaken you slowly?"

Her lungs hitched. "Cheater. You've played this game before."

She felt his mouth turn up against her cheek. "Let's assume I'm a quick study. Your answer? I believe that was three questions."

"It was?"

Who was seducing whom here? And how far did she want this to go? Never had she contemplated such a dangerous liaison with a mysterious man she'd only just met but who touched her on so many levels.

"Bed, shower or asleep? I must know in order to tell you what I plan to do. Or perhaps you'd prefer I show you?"

Yes, yes she would. Except she couldn't speak, as he slid an arm around her waist, drawing her taut against his warm body. She clutched his shoulders and they were amazing and strong underneath his jacket. "There's no shower on this balcony."

"So true," he murmured. "The alarm's going off."

It wasn't. She didn't care.

He covered her mouth with his and turned her into liquid

mercury for the second time. The man was a master, hot and forceful, and her lips fell open under the divine pressure. He plunged in, tongue skimming against hers, deliciously rough and tasting of champagne.

She moaned and changed the angle, inviting him deeper, urging him forward with small tugs of her hands against his shoulders. *More*, she needed more, needed to quench the thirst raging in her veins with this extremely arousing man.

Judging by the full-fledged blaze between them, he felt the same. About *her*, not Eva. How great was that, to be with a man who hadn't already made a bunch of snap judgments?

"Touch me," she commanded hoarsely, her damaged voice even more raw with desire.

Almost hesitantly, he palmed her breast through the thick bodice of the dress, and she nearly growled in frustration. Forget that. She reached down and gathered up the hem of the ridiculously full skirt and tucked it under the sash at her waist. She guided his hand through the opening, straight to her bottom.

It was his turn to groan as he flattened his palm against her bare cheek. "A thong? That is unbelievably sexy."

"Not nearly as sexy as your hand on it while I'm still fully dressed." He explored the uncovered flesh and traced the strings into her crevice and back out again. Her knees almost buckled. "Don't stop. Keep going."

He took her mouth again, ravenous and greedy, as his fingers nudged underneath the silk. Just far enough to steal her breath for a long second. Blatantly, she circled her pelvis, silently begging him to go deeper.

Whether she'd planned to go this far or not, her body wasn't holding back. She was about to come apart under his capable hands.

Instead, he withdrew entirely and blew out a heavy breath, smoothing her skirts down with a confusing finality. "Angie, I have to confess something."

"You're married." Disappointment swamped her so quick

and so fast she nearly convulsed. The ache, which had moments ago been a vortex of desire, cooled. She should have known.

"No." He shook his head in vehement denial. "I'm completely unattached. It's just…I don't…"

"You're not attracted to me." But his impressive length had ground hard against her, evident even through the monstrosity of fabric at her waist.

He swallowed hard. "How could you possibly think that? I've never been so turned on in my life. There's this one small problem. I've never seduced a woman on a balcony, so I'm ah…unprepared."

Oh. "You don't have a condom."

The giggle slipped out before she could stop it. He was just so flustered and so cute, running a hand over his dark blond hair with evident frustration. It caught her quite unexpectedly in a soft, warm place inside. Talk about being unprepared.

Was he ever going to stop being so unexpected and amazing? God, she hoped not.

Three

"I'm glad you find my lack of preparation amusing." Matthew certainly didn't. He'd never been so mad at himself and so happy she wasn't angry, all at the same time.

And he had never been in quite so much physical pain. Yes, the women in his social circle were sophisticated and demure, rightly so, but lukewarm in their approach to everything.

He never realized how truly hot it could be with someone so uninhibited.

"It's not funny. Trust me, it's not." She pulled him down by the lapels and kissed him sweetly. "That's for not having a condom."

"What?"

She shrugged with a delicate one-shoulder move. "I've been around my share of dogs. It's nice to find someone who isn't always thinking with what's in his pants. Besides, this isn't the dark ages. You can easily be mad at me for not having one."

"I take it that means you don't."

She shook her head. "And I can't do birth control. Everything gives me headaches. But we're in luck because it's

Carnevale. I bet we can score a boxful of very festive condoms from Vincenzo's room."

So now Matt had been reduced to stealing condoms. Brilliant. Condoms were not first and foremost on his mind, yet he'd gladly jumped into her wicked game without hesitation.

What was he doing on this balcony?

"Maybe it's a sign."

"A sign? Like what, we're not supposed to hook up tonight?"

Hook up. Matthew Wheeler did not *hook up*. He'd been happily married to the perfect woman and would still be if an aneurism hadn't killed her. Commitment made him tick.

Angie might discount the idea of signs, but he couldn't. This wasn't meant to happen and probably for a very good reason. Did he really want a one-night stand with some woman he'd met at a party? It just wasn't his style.

The empty palazzo next door called his name, offering a place to retreat and lick his wounds. Where he would go to bed alone, dream about Amber and wake in a cold sweat. If he slept. Sometimes he lay awake, racked with remorse over leaving his family in the lurch.

That was his real life. This interlude with a winged woman at a masked ball was nothing but a fantasy born of desperation and loneliness. It wasn't fair to use Angie to appease either.

But God Almighty, it was difficult to walk away from her. When she'd been in his arms, pliant and sizzling, he heard the distinct sound of his soul waking up.

Angie's kiss-stung lips and luminous brown eyes nearly did him in. She'd asked him to be her fake boyfriend at this party, a role he'd stepped into with ease and enthusiasm, but without really considering what enormous pain must have driven her to ask.

He couldn't abandon her.

Matthew might not hook up, but neither did he have to listen to Matt, who despite Angie's belief, was very much thinking with the bulge in his pants. He needed to cool down and evaluate his goal here before he got carried away by the fantasy.

So he'd split the difference.

"Let's dance."

Wary surprise wrinkled her mouth. "At the party?"

"Sure. Why not? You haven't had a chance to throw your new boyfriend in lover boy's face yet." Neither of them had done much spelling-it-out and some clarity might be in order. "And I'd like to take a step back. Make sure we're both headed in the same direction."

"I hear you. The balcony *is* cold and I do like to dance," she mused. "How about this? I'll dart into Vincenzo's room and stuff my clutch with as many condoms as it'll hold. We'll dance. If you move to music like you do on a speed date, we'll be headed in the same direction all right—back upstairs and into my bed."

His pants grew tighter. Exactly how many times did she envision having sex? He shook his head to clear the erotic images she'd sprung loose in his brain. It didn't work.

"I'll consider myself warned."

She smiled and it was a whole lot wicked.

Matthew took her hand and led her toward what promised to be a provocative round of dancing. At least in a room full of people, the temptation to dive under Angie's skirt would be lessened.

If he did that again, he'd like to be much more clear-headed about it.

Unbelievably, more people had gathered in the rooms downstairs, filling the dance floor to overflowing. Couples swayed and dipped to the slow song. Matthew drew Angie into the sea of dancers, carefully navigating to protect her wings. He hadn't danced in a long time but the ballroom classes he'd let Amber drag him to came back in a rush.

He positioned his arms and prepared to try some semblance of a modified waltz, or at least do the best he could in such a crowd. Angie melted against him, undulating her hips against his in a hypnotic, sensual rhythm. A hot lick of need coursed through his gut. She hadn't attended the same classes. Obviously.

He held her close, mimicking her moves. All he could think about was the scrap of silk underneath her skirt. And the foil packets rounding the sides of her clutch. He wasn't doing a very good job of splitting the difference.

Angie's ear was right by his mouth, and he had the most insane urge to nibble on it. Instead, he cleared his throat to ease the knot of sexual tension that had stiffened everything in his body.

"What if we continue our speed date but take it down a notch?"

She repositioned her head so it was lying in the hollow of his shoulder. The feathers anchored in her hair brushed across his neck. "I'm listening."

"What's your favorite color?"

"That's more like forty-seven notches. I don't have a favorite color. I like the rainbow." Someone bumped into her, shoving them closer together, not that he minded. "What's yours?"

The smell of her hair weakened his knees. Outside, it hadn't been so noticeable, but in the close, heated confines of the room, the exotic scent curled through his nose. Even her shampoo was unearthly, as if he needed another reminder they came from different worlds.

"Black. It goes with everything."

"How practical. I like that in a man. Where were you born?"

"Dallas. And please don't ask me if I've met J. R. Ewing. I've never been to Southfork, and I don't watch the TV show." That was one constant about Europe. Everyone knew Dallas from either reruns of the old drama or the reboot version on cable. "What about you?"

"Toronto. My mom moved to Detroit when I was a baby and became a U.S. citizen. That's where I grew up."

So maybe their worlds weren't as far apart as he'd assumed. "You're American?"

The silence stretched long enough for Matthew to wonder if he'd said something to offend her. But she had to know her ragged voice didn't carry a discernible accent and was unusual enough to warrant such a question.

"I'm nothing and everything," she said with a laugh that wasn't a laugh. "Usually I tell people I'm French Canadian. But I haven't been to Toronto in years. Or Detroit for that matter."

"Is your mom still in Detroit?"

"She lives in Minneapolis, for now, working on her fourth marriage. I have fam—other people in Detroit."

Other people? He didn't ask. The undercurrent of pain in her voice had been strong, and if she'd wanted him to know, she'd have said.

"Your home is in Europe then?"

"Or wherever the wind takes me." She injected a note of levity, but he wasn't fooled. Nowhere felt like home and it bothered her. "Do you still live in Dallas?"

"No." Lack of a home was something they shared. He'd sold his house, his car, everything. The only possessions he had to his name were the clothes in the closet at the palazzo and a few childhood mementos stored in his parents' extra bedroom. "I'm going where the wind takes me, too."

At least until he found the way home.

She stopped dancing and collided with the next couple, earning a dirty look from them. Impatiently, she pushed Matthew off the dance floor toward the side wall and peered up through her mask, eyes liquid with sympathy. "I'm sorry."

"For?"

"For whatever happened."

She didn't question him,, though she could obviously read between the lines as well as he could.

A wave of understanding rippled between them. Both of them were searching. Both of them carried secrets full of pain and misery and loneliness.

They weren't different at all.

She whispered, "I'm glad the wind blew us to the same place."

All pretense of speed dating evaporated. Something much more significant was happening.

"Me, too."

Amber's death had broken his heart, nearly broken him entirely, and he couldn't fathom feeling that strongly about anyone else. For months and months, he'd despaired of ever feeling *anything* again, and like a foghorn echoing through the mist of his grief, this gravelly-voiced fantasy had appeared.

She was a gift, one he wasn't ready to give back.

No, he didn't want a one-night stand with some random woman, but he couldn't resist exploring what two damaged souls might become to each other.

With his brain firmly in command, he drew her hand into his and smiled.

"Instead of directions upstairs, I have a better idea. Come home with me."

Home. Evangeline liked the sound of it. She'd never had a home.

She'd had new stepfathers every few years. A half sister, Lisa, whom their father had obviously preferred since he'd married Lisa's mother. Plenty of hotel rooms and airplanes—all of that, she'd had.

She wished she could indulge in something so simple, so achingly honest as *home.* But imagine if she took off her mask and Matt turned out to be a reporter. Or worse.

At Vincenzo's, masks were part of the ambience, the anonymity. Masks kept things surface level. Masks kept a man at arm's length and promised nothing more than one night, a brief, sizzling interruption of loneliness. Masks prevented rejection. And scars. She'd had enough of both, thanks.

And there was no doubt Matt had a couple of his own scars.

With a light laugh, she blinked at him coquettishly. "What are you proposing?"

"A continuation. No exes. No crowds. No rules. Just me and you and whatever feels right."

Oh. That might be okay. "What if I wanted to keep our masks on? What would you say?"

"No rules. For anything."

Her insides shuddered deliciously. "That's a little open-ended. How do I know you aren't into some very naughty things?"

"You don't. We're both taking a leap of faith."

The wicked gleam in his eye didn't reassure her, but it certainly piqued her interest. "I might be into naughty things."

"I'm counting on it." He tugged her hand as the music switched to another electronic number. The crowd went crazy, pressing in on them from all sides. "Come on."

To her left, she glimpsed Sara Lear posing for a picture with two men in drag. Rory was nowhere in sight, but he might pop up again at any moment. That decided it. The last thing she wanted was to be at this party alone, constantly reminded of how she wasn't Sara.

Matt was clearly lonely, too. She'd head in his direction and see where it led.

"Let's go. Right now."

He kept her hand in his and led her out of Vincenzo's palazzo via a side entrance. They crossed a moonlit courtyard and climbed an ornate outer staircase to the second floor. Matt held the door for her to enter ahead of him. Lights flashed.

"Welcome to Palazzo D'Inverno," he said.

Evangeline's breath stalled in her throat. Relief frescos lined the walls and extended to the ceiling, where the colors exploded into Renaissance-style art of unparalleled beauty. Modern terrazzo floors studded with chips of marble and granite spread underneath her feet and met three sets of glassed French-doors leading to what appeared to be a marble balcony overlooking the Grand Canal.

Three long leather sofas in sea-foam green formed a U in the center of the living room, and all three afforded an amazing view of Venice, lit for Carnevale with breathtaking splendor.

"This is unbelievable." There were no other words. Vincenzo's palazzo had been in his family since the time of the Medici but it couldn't hold a candle to this one. "I had no idea anything like this still existed in Venice."

Matt's mouth twisted into a semblance of a smile. "Keeps the rain out."

"Whoever owns this place hit the jackpot. You're lucky they agreed to rent it out. It's amazing."

He shot her a quizzical look. "I'll be sure to pass on the compliment."

"Do you have all three floors, or just the *piano nobile*?"

"Top two. The bottom floor isn't restored. The bedrooms are upstairs. Would you like to see them?"

"Was that a line?" She grinned at his chagrined expression. He was endearing in a way that shouldn't be possible in conjunction with his forceful, compelling personality. "If so, I must say it worked extraordinarily well. I not only want to see the rest of the house, purely for aesthetic reasons of course, but I want to get out of this dress in the worst way."

She took a step toward the twisting staircase, but he tugged her back and pierced her with his beautiful crystalline eyes, capturing her gaze with his and refusing to let her go.

"Angie, I didn't invite you here solely to get you naked.

When I said no rules, I meant no expectations. If nothing happens, that's all right. I don't mind if we talk until dawn. Whatever feels right. Remember that."

"Matt—" The rest froze in her throat.

He was nothing like the people in her world. He carried a hint of vulnerability, a depth that pulled at her. And his restraint—that she couldn't fathom. All the men she knew took what they wanted, when they wanted it.

Not this one. He was very clearly telling her she still had choices, regardless of how brazenly she'd thrown herself at him all night. He didn't just see her as an outlet to slake his thirst but as a valued companion. That was powerful. And seductive.

She whispered his name again. "I don't mind if we talk, either."

She never talked. Talking sucked, especially when the sound of her own voice made her cringe. But they both deserved to have choices.

"Is that what you want?"

She craved the attention of this man, who seemed to understand exactly what she needed, when she needed it. To understand the weight of loss and the pain of being adrift, desperate for an anchor.

Something momentous swelled in her chest. "I just want to be with you."

"You've got me. For however long you'd like. I'm not going anywhere." As if to prove it, he lowered the lights, creating a romantic ambience instantly. He sat on the couch and spread his hands. "Think of me as a smorgasbord."

She laughed, and it blew away all the thick implications of the moment.

"Now that's something I've never had before. By the way, I wasn't kidding about getting out of this dress. I can hardly breathe, and it's heavy."

"Would you like a T-shirt?"

"Um, not really. What I'd really like is your help." She

stepped out of her heels, crossed the room and sat on the couch facing away from him. "The laces in the back are too hard to reach."

"What would you have done if we hadn't connected? Slept in it?"

Connected. That hit her in all the soft, warm places again. This was a connection, a greater one than she'd been looking for, or had expected, and far more precious—thanks to the custom of wearing masks for Carnevale. She'd never have let her guard down otherwise.

"I would have figured out something," she murmured as he gently lifted her curls and swept them up over her shoulder. Her skin prickled as she felt his gaze on the bare expanse from her hairline to the strapless bodice.

His hands skimmed down her back on either side of the wings, stoking the fire he'd built on the balcony, which hadn't extinguished at all. Those strong fingers pulled on the threads, unknotting them and drawing them through the grommets with deliberate, aching leisure.

She kept expecting to feel his lips on her shoulder, on the column of her neck, or at the place where fabric met her skin. But the longer he held back, and the longer her skin burned for his touch, the crazier it drove her.

Yes, he was a master at this anticipation game. Among other things. When she finally got him naked and under her, she'd show him a thing or two.

Except she still wasn't sure they were headed for the bedroom. It was disorienting to have her temporary, surface-level liaison morph into something undefinable. Something so much more than a quick fix for loneliness.

So what was it?

Finally, after an eternity, the laces pulled free from the bodice, loosening the corset and spilling her breasts partially over the neckline of the dress, and he still hadn't made a move.

"It, uh, has to come over my head," she said without turning around. She raised her arms. "Can you…?"

He grasped the bodice but she was sitting on the skirt, so she wiggled and he pulled, until the yards and yards of lace tulle eased past her waist. The mask popped up onto her forehead, but she repositioned it before the skirt fully came off.

Then she was naked except for her thong. And the mask. What would he do first? The way he'd answered that question back on the balcony had been maddeningly vague.

He draped her dress over the back of the couch. She faced the canal, away from Matt, and he had yet to say a word. Screaming sexual tension whipped through all her nerves until she thought she'd pass out.

"So. What did you want to talk about?"

His soft laugh settled inside her. "I'm wondering about this."

He traced the trail of eight notes tattooed in a string at the small of her back. The smooth touch unleashed a tremor she couldn't control. "It's a tattoo."

"The notes are all the colors of the rainbow. I like it."

No one had ever noticed that before. "Music is important to me."

It was more than she'd meant to say and communicated none of the shock of pure grief the words had unearthed. She shoved the grief back, like she always did, shoved back the longing for a voice to express the pain. If she had a voice, she'd have no pain to express. It was a cruel, vicious circle she couldn't escape.

Except this was one night she didn't have to face the darkness alone. "Matt."

"Angie."

The smile in his voice warmed her. "Just making sure you're still there. Are we going to talk some more or is there something you'd like to do instead?"

"Was that a line?"

"Yes. It was." The ache at her core spread, and only the man behind her could ease it. She'd never wanted to be with someone more. What did she have to do to get him to make a move? "Obviously not a good one since you're still sitting there like yo—"

"Stand up and turn around, Angie."

She did slowly.

His hooded gaze swept her from head to toe, lingering along the way and unleashing a delicious tingle in all the places his eyes touched.

"You are the most beautiful woman alive. Come here."

He grasped both her hands and stood to meet her. In one breath, he drew her into his arms and kissed her.

Flames exploded at their joined mouths, between their bodies, crackling down the length of her bare skin where the soft fabric of his suit brushed it. Oh, how wrong she'd been. He *was* a man who took what he wanted. And he wanted to consume her whole.

She wanted to let him.

They *connected*. On every level.

When he tilted her head back to access her throat with his firm, gorgeous mouth, their masks caught at the corners. Patiently, he disentangled them and glanced down into her eyes, suddenly still. "No expectations. Does this feel right?"

Without warning, he skated a hand down her spine and fanned it at the small of her back, cradling the tattooed music notes in his capable hand as if he knew he held her very center.

Her eyelids fell closed and she moaned. "More right than anything I've ever felt. Please don't say you're really in the mood to talk."

He laughed against her throat, and she felt the caress of his lips clear to her toes. "I'm not. But I would be happy to talk, if that's what you wanted."

She shook her head almost imperceptibly, terrified she'd dislodge his mouth from her skin. "I want you."

"Good. Because I'm about to make love to you."

Yes, she wanted that, too. To be filled by this very different man, to the brim. To connect, bodies and minds. Souls.

He threaded a hand through the hair at her neck, his fingers solid and firm against it. "Angie," he murmured, almost reverently.

"Stop." Tears stung the corners of her eyes. Baffling, irrepressible tears because she wanted something else from him, something she'd resisted all evening. "Just stop."

"Okay." His hands withdrew and the sudden lack of support buckled her knees.

"No! Don't stop touching me. Stop calling me Angie." Before her subconscious could come up with one of the hundreds of reasons it was a dangerous idea, she reached up and yanked off her mask. "My name is Evangeline. Make love to *me*, not the mask."

Four

"Evangeline."

It flowed from Matthew's mouth like a prayer. Yes. *That* fit this angelic, winged woman who had bared herself to him in more ways than one.

He drank in her face, and it jolted something inside, as if his soul had done a double take and said, *There you are*.

"Angie is a nickname. Evangeline is who I am."

A nameless emotion tightened his throat. "I'm honored you trusted me with it."

She'd done far more than simply remove her mask. The significance of it sent a flood of guilt through him. Guilt because he could shed his physical mask—but not his internal one.

And still he drew off his mask and dropped it to the floor. "Allow me to reciprocate."

For a long while, she fixated on his face. His neck heated. Who would have thought taking off a mask could provoke such intensity?

"God, you're gorgeous."

"Most people call me by my given name, but if you want to address me as God, I won't argue."

She laughed, pushing her firm breasts into his chest. "Way to defuse the moment. That's a rare talent."

He'd intended to diffuse his own embarrassment at her frank admiration, which even Amber had expressed infrequently. But if Evangeline chose to believe he had superpowers, so much the better.

"Are we finished with the revelations?" he asked.

"Not even close. Now that I've seen what's under that mask, I'm dying to peel away this suit—" she flicked his bow tie "—and get a look at the rest of the goods."

"I hope it meets with your expectations." His voice dropped. Nerves. Of all things.

Before fully internalizing the implications, he swept Evangeline into his arms and carried her up the stairs to the bedroom.

"Any man who can do that without having to catch his breath most definitely has a body that'll meet my expectations," she said as he laid her on the bed. "Oh, wow. That's quite a fresco."

Matthew glanced up at the ceiling, where stucco divided sixteen individual paintings last touched by a brush during the Renaissance. "It's my favorite."

"I like it, too. I'll lie here and look at it while you fetch the condoms out of my clutch. Which is downstairs." She flipped him a cheeky grin as he cursed.

He cursed some more as he tromped back down the narrow stairs in search of the errant bag. It was still attached to her dress, but instead of pulling out a couple of condoms—because who was he to question how many they'd need—he untied it and brought the whole thing.

The bulging sides of Evangeline's clutch induced a healthy dose of reality. He was about to have sex with a virtual stranger, one whose face he'd seen for the first time less than ten minutes ago. Halfway up the stairs, he paused.

Was he really going to go through with this?

It was one night. One night in which he had an opportunity to turn the tide of his grief and rejoin the living by spending time with a beautiful woman who made him feel ten feet tall—feel being the operative word. One night when he could act recklessly with no one the wiser. He was in the most romantic city in the world, perhaps on purpose, and he wanted all that Venice had to offer.

Evangeline was draped across the cream-colored comforter when he strode through the bedroom door. She studied the ceiling with pursed lips, hair spread out underneath her and breasts freely on display. That lack of inhibition—it staggered him. Excited him.

His body hardened in anticipation, and his fingers tingled as he recalled the smoothness of her bare skin. This one night was a rare offer from the universe, and he was incredibly lucky to get it.

She glanced over with a sultry smile. "You. Come here."

Only a fool would pass up what was clearly fate.

With one hand, he got rid of his shoes and socks as he crossed the room. He tossed her clutch on a pillow and stared at her gorgeous form, flawless in the lamplight. "Hold on a minute."

He pulled a book of matches from his bedside drawer and lit the candles lining ornate sconces on each side of the bed, then clicked off the light.

"Nice. You could have gotten me here a lot faster if you'd said that was the first thing you'd do once I'm naked." She sat up and grasped his lapels, drawing off his jacket with a quick yank. "And you have on too many clothes. I'm feeling self-conscious here."

He let the jacket fall to the floor. "I can't imagine why. You're beautiful."

Flames flickered over her skin and threw honey highlights into her curls.

Her hands, which had been busy with his tie, rested flat on his chest, and she rose up on her knees to meet his gaze.

A hundred emotions poured from her expression, passing between them in silent communication.

"You know why," she said.

He did. In her eyes, he saw the same things she no doubt saw in his. They had an understanding, nonverbal and mystifying, but very real. He'd felt it from the first moment in the hall. He felt it now.

She was self-conscious not because of her nakedness, but because she'd removed her mask and feared learning she'd made a mistake in trusting him.

This night was about two damaged people seeking a port in the storm. He was going through with it because he wanted to live up to her trust. Wanted to fall into a woman so different from any he'd ever met, one so wrong for a real estate broker from Dallas, but perfect for a man who didn't know who he was or how to live his life anymore.

He wanted to see what happened if he let go of all the rules. It couldn't be worse than the purgatory of the past eighteen months.

If he did it right, it would be spectacular. Meaningful. And Matthew did *everything* right.

"I'm not going to disappoint you," he said hoarsely.

"I know. I wouldn't be here otherwise." Her voice had grown impossibly huskier as well, skating across his skin, burrowing its gravelly hooks into his center. "I've just never done anything like this before. Never wanted to."

Well, that made two of them. Hopefully they could figure it out together. "No expectations. No rules."

"I remember. Except I have this one rule." She made short work of removing his bow tie and began slipping his shirt's buttons free with deliberate care as she peeked up from under her lashes. "I get to explore first. You have to wait your turn."

He went so hard, his spine curved. Had a woman ever undressed him so provocatively?

"That's a pretty unfair rule. Why can't we do it at the same time?"

"Because I said."

The last button popped from its mooring, and she slid blazing fingertips across his bare chest on her way to his shoulders. His shirt came off in her hands and she yanked it halfway down his arms, trapping them against his side.

"Actually," she added, "the rule states I get to explore twice, once with my eyes and another time with my mouth."

Said eyes roamed over his exposed skin as she pulled him closer with the grip she had on his shirt. Without warning, she spun him and tied his hands behind his back with the fabric.

"Oh, now that's *really* not fair."

"All's fair in love and war." Still on her knees, she turned him back around to graze a fingertip down his chest and into the waistband of his pants. "I'll let you go when I'm done exploring."

She drew him closer and dropped his pants and briefs to the floor, ravishing his erection with her eyes, as promised.

He kicked his pants away. "I can easily break out of this you know."

"You won't." Her light tone fooled him not in the least.

This was love *and* war. And holy cow, did that get his juices flowing in a way he'd never have guessed. He'd play along, but she better believe he'd be dishing it out when he got the chance.

With a soft sigh, she twirled her finger. "Turn around. I want to see it all."

He faced the wall opposite the bed, slightly uncomfortable and enormously turned on by the notion of her eyes traveling up and down his naked body.

"When does the mouth exploration start?" he called over his shoulder.

Her answer came with a soft touch at the base of his

spine. Hair brushed his skin as she nibbled upward and his long-neglected body erupted with heat.

By the time she reached his neck, her tongue had joined the party. He groaned at the wicked swipe of wet heat against his earlobe, and allowed her to spin him slowly as she followed the line of his jaw with her lips.

Then there was no more talking as she kissed him.

He wanted to drag her into his arms and respond in kind. But he couldn't. His honor forced him to stay constrained as she did her best to drive him mad. He spiraled closer to the edge as she tilted his head in her palms to take the kiss deeper, teasing her nipples across his chest in a tantalizing back-and-forth dance.

Evangeline broke the kiss, arching her back sensuously. The silk of her thong brushed his length, and he nearly came apart right then and there.

No. He breathed heavily through his nose and clamped down on his reaction.

"Matt," she breathed into his ear, and the low croak was the sexiest thing he'd ever heard. "When I first saw you, I noticed those capable hands. I want them on my body. Now."

She reached around to pull the knot of his sleeves apart, but he'd already yanked his wrists free.

His mouth was on hers instantly as he slid both palms down the heat of her back to cup her bottom. Smooth. Arousing. He crushed her against his erection and plunged into sensation, freely allowing his body to revel in the impressions, the awareness. Finally, he felt something other than frozen and disoriented.

As he dipped underneath the triangle of silk at her thighs, she moaned and strained forward, seeking his fingers, throwing her head back in pleasure.

That was as arousing as the feel of her skin.

She was nothing like Amber.

He willed away the comparison—ghosts had no place here. But the thought circled and grew. Amber had been sophisticated, elegant. Beautiful in the way of a glass swan with special handling requirements.

He'd always held her in slight reverence as the future mother of his children, and they'd shared a strong relationship anchored by common interests and goals. Their love life had blossomed into something wonderful and good. But conducted in the dark, under the sheets, which Matthew never minded.

This was something else, something erotic and animalistic and wicked. Evangeline wasn't Amber. And there were no rules tonight.

He wanted to bury himself in this woman and be resurrected a new man.

Evangeline enfolded Matt with her arms and willed him to hurry. But there was no rushing the man she'd been goading with tied hands for the past few minutes.

His fingers wrapped her in a veil of pleasure as they slowly traveled across her skin, spinning magic through her center as he touched her everywhere—inside and out.

Yes. Exactly what she needed—to be filled, valued, appreciated. Accepted.

With incredible restraint, he lowered her to the mattress and drew off her underwear, then crawled up the length of her body, laving every inch of skin as he went. He reached her throat and tilted her head back to taste with hard suction. Simultaneously, his thigh separated hers, relentless against her sensitized flesh and setting off pyrotechnics behind her eyes.

She'd never dropped into such heavy desire so quickly, never been so hot and ready to explode. Usually it took a while. But then, they'd been engaged in foreplay in one form or another since their first meeting in the hall.

Was it any wonder Matt was about to take her under with only his thigh?

His tongue circled her breasts, then treated her to the

same intense suction he'd used on her throat. Her back came off the bed, arching, as her feminine parts contracted. She gasped.

"Now, Matt."

It was supposed to be a demand, not a plea. But the words left her lips on a broken sob, and she no longer cared that a man had reduced her to begging.

He extracted a condom and fingered it on. It took an eternity but then he was back between her thighs, sliding into her. Watching her as they became one and their gazes locked. Something powerful, divine even, swelled between them and her heart thumped in time with the throb in the air.

No, she'd never done this before because she had no idea what *this* was.

It certainly wasn't a random hookup. But neither was it safe. The deeper the connection, the deeper the eventual pain.

She'd taken off the mask in a calculated gamble, and Matt hadn't recognized her. It should have allowed her to simply revel in this one night where a man couldn't hurt her because he didn't really know her. It should have been freeing. Not confusing.

Desperately, she cast about for a way to eliminate the swirling mass of vulnerability this man evoked by simply looking at her. Through her.

"Not this way." She wiggled and he rolled to his side, confusion evident.

"Too soon?"

"Too missionary." Waggling her brows, she knelt on the bed and glanced back at him. "Try this on for size."

He grinned and instantly heated her back with his torso, mouth to her neck as he filled her again from behind. Much better. Now she couldn't see all that depth of emotion. And vice versa. They'd pleasure each other and stave off the loneliness for a night and go on.

His fingers teased her flesh. Clearly this was not his first rodeo. She let her senses flood with Matt and moaned as he lit her up expertly. His name fell from her lips and too late she realized it didn't matter if she could see his face. His touch conveyed more depth than she'd dreamed possible.

Tears pricked her eyelids. She wanted that touch to mean everything she sensed it did. But was terrified to admit it. How could she convince herself this was nothing but a brief divergence if he kept touching her that way?

The orgasm, quick, powerful and amazing, swallowed her whole long about his second thrust, and he exploded with his third.

She collapsed, chest to the bed, and he spooned her into his arms, both of them still shuddering. He held her tightly and she curled into him, shocked at how natural it felt, how right, when normally she preferred not to be touched as her body cooled.

"I have never come so fast in my life," she gasped. "I think that's my new favorite position."

Though somehow, it hadn't been quite the cure for her confusion that she'd envisioned. And lying here in his arms with his thumb tenderly stroking the curve of her waist wasn't helping. The powerful flames of desire he fanned weren't sexual. She wanted Matt to be different. Special.

She should get dressed and leave. Right now, before she found out he wasn't.

But if she left, what then? Spend the rest of the night alone, huddled in the dark, listening to Vincenzo's guests party till dawn?

"It's definitely my new favorite position." He cleared his throat. "Though I'm willing to try a couple of others to verify. In a few minutes. I know we have all these condoms, but you're not an easy woman to recover from."

She had to smile at that. Nice to know it had been staggering on both sides.

A part of her had prepared to be kicked out. Maybe hoped she would be—it was safer that way. Not all men liked a woman hanging around afterward. Finding out Matt didn't fall in that category thrilled her. Dangerously.

"What if we just talk?"

Where had that come from? She never stayed.

She nearly took it back, but her soul ached, and Matt inexplicably salved it. Morning was soon enough to escape. For now, she wanted one whole night of fantasy, where nothing mattered but being with a man who liked her and wanted her around.

His lips curved up against her temple. "A continuation of our speed date?"

The chilly palazzo air raised goose bumps on her arms. "Well, I'm not sure how we could find any more levels of compatibility. But okay."

He laughed. "Yeah, we gel. At least in bed, which is fantastic. It's been a while."

"Really? How long?"

Rolling her gently to the side, he pulled the covers free and nestled her back in his arms underneath them, like he'd read her mind. "A year and a half. Or so."

Oh, God. "Are you like, religious or something? Did I make you break vows?"

"No." He was quiet for a long time. "That's when my wife died."

Something hot exploded in her chest. His pain—she'd seen it, knew it was there, but never would have guessed its roots went so deep.

"Oh, Matt. I'm so sorry."

She rolled and took his lips with hers in a long kiss of sympathy. Why, she didn't know. It wasn't like she could fix anything or erase his agony, not with a million kisses.

"Thanks," he whispered against her lips. "It was a long time ago."

Her heart hurt for him and furiously demanded she find a way to salve his soul in return. "There's no statute of limitations on being sorry that someone you loved is gone."

"I guess not." His smile flipped her stomach. "When you said *talk,* that's probably not what you meant. But I thought you should know."

Because there was something more here than either of them had expected. He felt it, too.

"That's why you're drifting. To find some sort of closure." His nod confirmed what she'd guessed. "You're not in Venice on business, are you?"

"I wish it was that simple. If only there was a way to close the deal on grief, I'd be all set."

Matt was a widower. It felt weird. "People our age shouldn't die."

People their age shouldn't lose a career over botched surgery either, but crappy things happened with no rhyme or reason.

He smoothed a curl away from her face, his expression unreadable, and she waited for a demand that she slice open a vein in kind, share her personal pain with him. She wouldn't. Couldn't. And it wasn't fair to Matt that he'd hooked up with someone nowhere near as willing to be vulnerable.

But he didn't hand her a scalpel.

"Are we the same age? Wait, am I allowed to ask that? Isn't there a rule about asking women their age?"

A laugh slipped out. "No rules, remember? I'm twenty-seven."

"Thirty-two." He grinned. "Not nearly old enough to need *that* long to recover."

She let him change the subject by kissing her breathless and rolling on top of her, bracing himself on his strong forearms. He met her gaze, his eyes full of her, not pain. They'd connected over their mutual search for a way to combat the darkness, and it was working.

For one magical night, they had each other.

Five

When Evangeline awoke, Matt was watching her, cheek to his pillow. The drapes were flung apart, and sunlight spilled into the room, across the bed. With strong features and those amazing blue eyes, he was more gorgeous by morning light than he was by candlelight.

"Hey there." He smiled and laced their fingers, bringing hers to his lips.

She smiled back. "If you're always this cheerful in the morning, you might want to keep sharp objects under lock and key."

With a laugh, he tucked a curl of her hair behind her shoulder. "I'm not this cheerful ever. You have the unique effect of being a good influence."

Or the unique effect of breaking his dry spell with women. The sunlight had returned her cynicism, apparently.

"Are you watching me for a reason or auditioning to be my stalker once the boyfriend job is over?"

"For a reason. But you'll think it's weird."

Her eyes narrowed. "Weirder than watching me while I sleep?"

"I like your face." He shrugged. "It was covered most of the night, and I haven't seen it nearly enough yet."

"There's nothing special about my face." Other than how famous it was. She sat up and threw off the covers, intending to flee before the discussion went in a direction she didn't like.

Besides, it was morning. She'd stayed long enough.

His hand shot out from under the sheet to grab her wrist and tug her back. "I could look at you for hours."

"I'm naked. Of course you could." *Men.* But his eyes weren't on her uncovered body.

She was trying so hard to assign typical male qualities to Matt, and he wasn't letting her.

"You still have feathers in your hair."

"I do?" Her hand flew to her hair and sure enough, a mess of pins still held part of her headpiece in place. Wonderful. Her hair must resemble a bird's nest after a monsoon.

"Let me."

He rose up from the cocoon of sheets, which fell from his body in a slow waterfall, and her belly contracted. There was very little typical about Matt, and his prime physique was no exception.

He scooted up behind her, but not close enough to touch. It didn't matter. His heat radiated outward, stroking her skin with delicious fingers of warmth. With aching gentleness, he plucked a pin from her hair, then another, his breath fanning her scalp as he worked.

Awareness prickled her skin and ignited a slow burn in her center.

"That was the last pin."

But his fingers stayed in her hair, combing it lightly, patiently untangling the snarls. Then his fingers drifted to her shoulders in a caress. He lifted her curls and touched the back of her neck with his warm, talented lips, unleashing an unexpected shiver.

She shouldn't stay. Her one magical night was over, and

morning light put a damper of reality over everything. In fact, she should have left before he woke up. Why hadn't she?

"Matt."

The lips paused in their trek across her nape. "Are you about to tell me you have somewhere to be? Nice knowing you, but party's over?"

Was she that easy to read? "I don't have anywhere to be."

Well, that was a stupid thing to admit. Now she had no exit strategy if she decided she needed one.

"Then don't go."

His hands gripped her arms, drawing her backward into him, supporting her with his chest as he ravished whatever he could reach with his mouth. Her insides erupted.

She wasn't going anywhere, not yet. But she also wasn't doing this backward. Not this time.

She spun in his arms and wrapped her legs around his waist. The delight playing with the corners of his mouth sent a shaft of heat through her. "Just try and get rid of me, cowboy."

His laugh rumbled against her flesh. "Not everyone from Texas rides horses."

"Who's talking about riding horses?" She shoved his chest and knocked him back against the comforter, moving onto her knees over him. "Giddyap."

Now there was a sight. Gorgeous, masculine magnificence spread underneath her thighs. Matt was hard all over, had a nicely defined torso and a wicked smile. She'd won the man sweepstakes and had been daft enough to miss out on watching him last night.

Eyes stormy with dark desire, he lifted his chin. "Your turn to fetch the condoms."

She stretched to pull one off the bedside table and ripped it open with her teeth. "Done."

"Then saddle up, sweetheart." He shoved his hands under

his head with a mischievous wink. "You don't have to tie me up this time."

Which she'd only done to ratchet down the emotion of the moment. It had failed miserably.

"Liked that, did you?"

The flippant response almost caught in her throat. Because she didn't want to be flippant. Didn't want fun and games. She wanted the tender, profound Matt of last night who made her feel cherished.

When had she turned into such a *girl*? Five minutes ago, she was halfway out the door—mentally, at least—and here she was wishing for the opposite. Matt had her completely messed up.

"I have yet to discover something about you I don't like," he said.

"I've got you good and fooled then."

He pierced her with the force of all that depth behind his eyes. "I don't think so."

She looked away, letting the condom fall to the bed. "You don't know me. Not really."

No one did—by design. How much worse would rejection hurt if someone dug through all the protective layers and exposed her core? Well, she already knew. It would feel an awful lot like when her dad hadn't wanted her.

"That's not true." He sat up, resettled her against his thighs and cupped her chin. "I recognized you as soon as you took off your mask."

Her heart plunged to the floor and tried to keep going. "You did?"

Why hadn't he said anything? Duh. He hadn't because he'd wanted to score with Eva. Of course. Disappointment nearly wrenched a sob from her frozen chest. He wasn't special. Big surprise.

"Something inside me did, as if I'd always known you." He shook his head with a half laugh. "Sorry. I'm no good at this, and to top it off I sound like a starry-eyed teenager. They must put romance in the water here."

"What are you saying?"

He huffed out a frustrated breath. "I don't know. I mean, it wasn't like, hey didn't we go to the same high school? It was an elemental recognition. Inside. Nothing like that has ever happened to me before." Matt's fathomless eyes begged her to understand, but she couldn't sort through the panic in her abdomen to put definition around his words. "I thought you felt it, too."

He meant that indefinable swirl between them. The *connection*.

Cautiously, slowly, her heart started beating again.

"The first time I kissed you. It didn't feel like the first time. Is that what you mean?"

He lit up, zinging her in the stomach. "Yes. That's it exactly. Everything between us…it's just right. We're sitting here naked having a conversation, and it's not strange."

The smile cracked before she registered that he'd pulled it from her. "Feels pretty good to me."

"Me, too. I know as much about you as I need to. You're my butterfly."

His lips claimed hers in a kiss full of promise. And like that, he turned the tables on her again, making her yearn for things she shouldn't, such as another night of absolving her loneliness in the arms of a man who wasn't eager to get rid of her. A man who made her feel valued.

If she stayed, how long could that possibly last?

The sooner she left, the sooner that yearning could dry up and blow away. But the second she walked out the door, she'd be back in the real world, lost and alone, with only the thin layer of Eva for protection—and that didn't go very far anymore.

Rock. Hard place.

With Matt, she was simply an anonymous woman enjoying the uncomplicated company of a man, and it gave her room to breathe she hadn't known she needed. One night hadn't been enough. But if she stayed, it was like giving Matt permission to get closer. That couldn't go well.

She stared into the depths of those almost-colorless-blue eyes.

A small voice in the back of her mind insisted she was selling this completely atypical man short.

Matthew palmed Evangeline's chin and kissed her until his brain sizzled. She was naked in his lap, legs around his waist, and the position was so sensually erotic, he was one rub of her flesh away from going off like a bottle rocket.

Last night had been a fantasy. This morning—still pretty unreal. He'd awoken with a start, afraid Evangeline had evaporated like so much mist in the sunlight. But there she was, hair draped over the pillow, breathing deeply in sleep, beautiful against his sheets. The way she filled his bed was so very nice.

Their one night was over. It wasn't enough, and he wasn't ready to say *ciao*.

Her hands cupped his butt, urging him closer and he was already almost inside her. One quick thrust and he would be. His thighs strained. He groaned against her mouth, blindly seeking the condom wrapper with clumsy fingers before it was too late.

His fingers closed around it, and he eased back a bit to roll it on, still kissing her because he couldn't stop.

Finally, it was in place. He lifted her bottom and slid in, all the way, and she breathed his name as he situated her flush against him.

His eyelids slammed closed as Evangeline washed through him, blasting away all the cobwebs until that incredible light of hers flooded the darkness inside. They moved together, heightening the pleasure, heightening the sense of completion until they both exploded simultaneously.

He wrapped his arms around her and held her tight

against his torso as the ripples went on and on. As they faded away, they left the warmest glow in their wake. His lips rested on her temple, and he couldn't have moved if his life depended on it.

"I like that position pretty well, too," she murmured, and he grinned.

"It has its merits." Her cheek rubbed his, bristling his morning stubble. As decadent as it was to still be in bed, they had to get up sometime. "Are you hungry? I'll make you breakfast."

It probably sounded as much like a stall tactic to her as it did to him. He didn't care. Too many things in his life had ended prematurely, and if she left, he'd probably never see her again. That would be a true shame.

"Do you mind if I take a shower first?" She made a noise. "I forgot, I don't have any of my stuff. Does the offer of a T-shirt still stand?"

"Sure. Give me a minute in the bathroom and then it's all yours." He eased her off his thighs and took shameless delight in watching his uninhibited butterfly roll onto her back, still breathing heavily.

Matthew pulled a T-shirt from the dresser and tossed it next to her on the bed. He bent down to kiss her thoroughly because he could, then whistled as he dressed and went downstairs to scare up some breakfast.

Whistled.

He'd be shocked, except his ability to be shocked had disappeared right around the time Evangeline had presented her naked backside and told him to hop on board. She was the most exciting woman he'd ever met, and under normal circumstances, real-estate mogul Matthew Wheeler would bore her instantly.

But this was Venice, and he was a guy who could keep up with Evangeline and talk about spiritual connections without flinching because there were no rules. Being Matt was liberating.

The updated plumbing in Palazzo D'Inverno only went so far, and when Evangeline turned on the shower upstairs, pipes rattled inside the kitchen walls. It was like music. His cold, lonely house was filled with Evangeline, and he liked it. A lot.

When she came downstairs clad in only his T-shirt, bare legs on display and wet hair dark against her shoulders, every drop of saliva in his mouth dried up.

"How do you make cotton look so good?"

He handed her a glass of orange juice.

"One of my natural talents."

She stood on her tiptoes to kiss him as if they were a couple comfortable in the kitchen dance from having performed it so many times. Sipping the juice, she perched on one of two stools at the center island and watched him at the stove.

"I hope eggs and toast are okay." He glanced over his shoulder and nearly dropped the spatula at the sight of such a tousled, stunning woman in his kitchen. "I guess I should have asked."

"It's fine. I don't do whacked-out diets or lament about animal rights. I just eat."

"I like that in a woman."

"I like a man who cooks."

They traded scorching hot glances until the scent of toast filled the air. He pulled it from the toaster and plated everything, then sat next to her at the island.

This was the first time he'd eaten a meal with a woman in…too long to recall. He'd missed the simple pleasure of awaking to warm female, of sharing a bathroom. Laughing and making love whenever the mood struck.

He missed being married, more than he'd realized. No amount of wishing, cursing, grieving or wandering could bring Amber back, though he'd irrationally tried it all. He could only embrace what *was* possible.

"So," he said after swallowing a bite of toast. "Do you have plans for the weekend?"

"It's Wednesday. The weekend is a long way off."

At home, his calendar filled months in advance and he lived by his schedule. In Venice, he'd learned calendars were a dirty word, which he still hadn't adjusted to. "I'd like to see you again. Maybe go on a date."

He definitely wasn't done with what Evangeline made him feel.

She put her fork down with all the fanfare of a royal announcement. "I'm not so big on dating."

"Oh." The brush-off. Apparently he was rustier at this than he'd realized, because he'd have sworn they had something going on here. "What are you big on?"

Her gravelly laugh surprised him. "You."

"Uh, okay." To stall, he shoveled food into his mouth and chewed slowly. His wits did not gather. "Can I assume you *are* that into me then?"

"Matt." She sighed, and it didn't reassure him. "You're the best thing that's happened to me in a long, long time. But—"

"Why does there have to be a *but?* I'm the best thing. Roll with that." He encouraged her with a finger twirl, unable to keep the grin off his face.

Negotiation time—his best skill. She was in for a surprise if she thought there was a chance in hell he was letting her get away.

Shoulders slumped, she stared at her plate for a long time. "What if I said I'd like to see you again too, but here? At your house?"

Her body language told him volumes about the importance of his answer.

He shrugged. "The last time I dated, dinosaurs roamed the earth. I'm not so big on it, either. I just want to see you. When? Pick a day that works for your life."

A firm commitment would settle the uneasiness prickling his spine quite well.

When she looked up from her plate, tears had gathered

and one slid down her face. A giant fist clenched his gut as she wiped away the tear.

"I don't have a life," she whispered.

"Evangeline…" What was he supposed to do? Say? Feel?

Instinctively, he slid from the stool, gathered her into his arms and held her, mystified, but happy to be doing *something*. She melted into him, her hands clutching his shoulders as if she couldn't get close enough, and he ached over her unidentified agony.

"I'm sorry. I don't usually fall apart in the middle of being asked out on a date." Her watery chuckle gave him hope things hadn't gone entirely to hell.

"I'm not asking you out on a date. No, ma'am. I have it on good authority you aren't big on dates. I'm asking you to my house for…dinner?" he offered, praying that would get a thumbs-up. "I'll cook."

"Dinner would be nice," she said into his shoulder. "Tonight. Tomorrow night. Any night."

"Tonight. In fact, just stay," he said, voicing the invitation he should have issued from the outset. This place needed her light. *He* needed it. "Unless you're sick of me or need to go hang out with Vincenzo since you're his guest."

"Vincenzo is probably sleeping off his hangover and won't notice if I'm there or not."

The forlorn note clinched it. Unless he'd completely lost his marbles, she wasn't ready to say *ciao,* either.

"I'll definitely notice if you're here or not. Italian TV leaves a lot to be desired, and I'd rather be with you. Spend another night, or better yet, through the weekend." The words rushed out before he'd hardly formed the thought, but the relevance of it, the weight of what he asked, was already there, inside him. He'd finally woken up from an eighteen-month stupor, and there was no way he'd let it end. "Will you stay?"

She hesitated, lids closed in apparent indecision. When

she opened her eyes, the flicker in their depths warned him something he might not like was about to happen.

"Why haven't you asked me about my voice?"

He blinked. "Was I supposed to?"

"It's damaged. Aren't you curious? You can't tell me you haven't noticed."

Damaged? It hadn't always been that way? "You noticed my hands and I noticed your voice. I love your voice. It's one of the sexiest things about you."

"It's not sexy. It's horrific, like a sixty-year old with a four-pack-a-day habit."

He laughed, but it didn't sound like he was amused. Because he wasn't. "That's ridiculous. Your voice is unusual. That's what makes it special. When you say my name, it latches onto me, right here." He grasped her hand and slapped it to his stomach. "I love that. I love that you can affect me by speaking."

She pulled her hand free. "You're being deliberately obtuse."

Frustrated, he shoved fingers through his hair. He'd invited her to draw out their one night, not solve world hunger—couldn't it be a simple yes or no?

"Fine. Evangeline, what happened to your voice?"

"When you sing a lot, polyps grow on your vocal cords. Sometimes they rupture. It requires a special expertise to perform the surgery to fix it. Adele had a good doctor. I didn't."

His brain nearly curdled at the lightning-fast subject change. "What's a lot? Like you sang professionally, you mean?"

"Yeah. Professionally. A lot." Her eyes searched his, hesitating, evaluating, and he got the impression she was feeling him out. They were still very much in the throes of negotiation, and he couldn't stumble now.

"No false pretenses," she said. "If I stay, I need you to know. When I sang, it was by another name. Eva."

"Eva."

The name flashed an image in his mind of the woman before him, but transformed into a lush, heavily made-up singer on stage in a tiny gold dress, with a hundred dancers weaving around behind her.

"Eva-who-performed-at-the-Super Bowl-Eva?"

She nodded, expression graveyard still as she waited for his reaction.

"Is that supposed to scare me?"

"I don't know what it's supposed to do. I just couldn't stand it being between us."

Matthew went cold. "Are you disappointed I didn't recognize you?"

When she'd removed her mask, he'd thought the jolt of recognition was uncanny. Had his subconscious simply remembered her from a halftime show?

The disappointment sharpened and stuck in his gut. Then faded abruptly. He'd felt something between them long before he saw her face.

"No, relieved." She clutched his hand. "My fame doesn't bother you? I have a lot of money. Does it change anything?"

"Not in the slightest."

She wasn't just wrong for Matthew Wheeler; she was in a whole other stratosphere of incompatibility, with a life full of limos, designer drugs and glittery celebrities. Hell, she *was* a glittery celebrity and glittery didn't gel with the blue bloods in his circles. But he'd realized they were wrong for each other five minutes after meeting, and though he desperately wanted to find a way to get back home, that wasn't happening today.

This was a finite Venetian affair, and Matt didn't care who she was. She made him feel alive for the first time in eighteen months, and that made her perfect for right this minute.

"Since we're going full bore on disclosures, I have money, too. I bought this palazzo as a wedding gift to Amber, my wife. In Dallas, I was a partner in a multimillion dollar real estate firm and drove an Escalade. Then I dumped all my responsibilities and jumped on a plane. I have little to offer anyone right now. Should I have told you that before we got involved? Does it change things for you?"

If it did, he wouldn't blame her. He was a bad bet emotionally.

"Is that what we are? Involved?" Some snap crept back into her eyes.

"Yeah. Wasn't looking for it, wasn't planning on it. I left Dallas to regain my sanity after my wife died, and I finally feel like that's possible, thanks to you." He slid a thumb down her jaw. "Stay."

"Matt," she whispered, and her palms came up to frame his face. "This is crazy. We just met."

"Tell me you're ready to walk away and I'll show you to the door."

She shook her head. Hard. "But you don't want to be seen in public with me. Someone always recognizes me. Then the harassment starts, rehashing how my career is over." Her eyes filled again. "It's not a lot of fun."

There was the source of all that anguish he'd sensed. This amazing, beautiful butterfly had been damaged beyond repair, and the public refused to let her forget. A fierce, protective instinct tightened his arms around her, filling him with a heavy impulse to do something to fix it for her, to help her.

They'd both lost something, and perhaps she needed him as much as he needed her, though she seemed much less willing to admit it.

In order to get her to stay—to give them *both* the peace they desperately sought—the terms might have to be less structured than he would like.

"Good. I don't want to go out. I don't want to share you." He gestured toward the room at large. "Inside these walls, we can block out the rest of the world and just be together. I need that. If you do too, then go to Vincenzo's, get your stuff and stay here for as long as that's true. When it's not, leave. No rules. No expectations."

It *was* crazy. And rash. So unlike a guy who missed his wife and valued commitment. That was the reason it worked, why he and Evangeline gelled, because he wasn't that guy right now.

Crazy was what made it great.

Six

Evangeline sneaked into Vincenzo's without stumbling over any passed-out revelers.

Once in her room, she threw on a sweater over Matt's T-shirt and stabbed her legs into jeans. Then she packed her suitcases in preparation for either the biggest mistake of her life or the smartest thing she'd ever done.

Jury was still out on which one Matt was. But she was willing to see what unfolded as they blocked out the world for a few days, especially with the caveat of his consent to leave whenever things got too stifling.

Roots weren't possible for someone like her, who fed from new experiences and new destinations. Who knew the dangers of staying in one place too long and allowing someone to matter. Being with a man who got that was huge.

So was the fact that he wasn't in a hurry to get rid of her.

When he'd asked her to stay, he still had no idea who she was—she could tell. And somehow, that had been the clincher. Eva ceased to have any relevance. Actually, it hadn't been a factor between them all along and she'd never had that. What started as a short-term anonymous encounter had accidentally turned into something else.

It was scary to be just Evangeline, scary to be so exposed, but deep inside, she yearned for someone to see beneath the layers and value *her*.

As soon as she found out Matt wasn't that someone, she'd be out the door.

In record time, she shut the lid on her second suitcase and zipped it. She had packing down to a science.

As she carried the suitcases down the marble staircase to Vincenzo's first floor, one of his buddies who'd passed out on the couch stirred. Franco. Or maybe it was Fabricio. He sat up and blearily evaluated her as he scrubbed his jaw.

"Eva. Didn't know you were here." A night of hard drinking slurred his accented English almost unintelligibly. He zeroed in on the suitcases. "Leaving already?"

"Yeah. Tell Vincenzo I said later."

"Wait. Do my show this week." He lifted his chin. "*Milano Sera* will treat you well."

She took in his too-handsome face and two-hundred-dollar haircut that not even a night of couch surfing could ruin. Now she remembered him. Franco Buonotti. He was the host of a late-night talk show on an Italian network. He'd bugged her a couple of times before to do an exclusive with him.

"I don't think so."

"Aww. Not even for me?" He batted his eyelashes, and she almost snorted.

Italian playboys were so not her type—she was more into blue-eyed blonds Regardless, she hadn't broken her silence on the botched surgery in six months and didn't see a reason to change that now.

"Not even."

She escaped to the haven her blue-eyed blond had offered.

Upstairs in Matt's bedroom, she unpacked her clothes and arranged them in the empty spots he'd cleared for her in the closet and dresser. Unable to resist, she opened a drawer to finger his shirts. Very few of his items lay folded inside or hanging in the closet. He traveled as light as she did. But then, neither of them had a permanent home.

Oddly, seeing their clothes mixed felt very permanent. It shouldn't have put a smile on her face.

Matt ordered lunch to be delivered, and the soup grew cold because they were too busy talking to eat. He was transparent and genuine, and his willingness to share covered her tendency not to. He never ran out of stories, and she forgot to be wary by the middle of the afternoon.

That's when *Milano Sera's* host intruded on her haven. Matt answered a knock at the door, and she glimpsed the too-handsome face of Vincenzo's friend through the crack.

"I'll take care of it," she told Matt and shooed him away from the door. "I already said no."

"*Cara*, no one says no to me."

He'd cleaned up and squeezed his impressive build into tight Dolce & Gabbana jeans and a distressed T-shirt. That kind of sexy might work on tittering schoolgirls, but Evangeline couldn't titter to save her life.

"Yet I did. This is a private home. Please respect that."

She shut the door in his face and turned to see Matt watching her.

"Sales guy?" he asked with raised eyebrows. "What was he selling? Ice to Eskimos?"

And somehow he pulled a smile from her. Matt's talents were amazing. "He hosts a talk show on an Italian network and wants me to do an interview."

"Badly, I guess, to chase you here."

"I'm sorry he bothered us." She sighed. "It was a nice idea, to block out the world. Unfortunately, the world tends to camp out on my doorstep."

With it came the intrusion of Eva…and a reminder of all the reasons she'd latched onto the suggestion of a place to hide. If she knew the answers to the questions, interviews might not be so hard.

Her phone beeped, as if to underscore the point. Like an

idiot, she checked it to see an apology text from Vincenzo. Well, that was something, at least.

Matt took the phone from her fingers and tossed it on the credenza to his left without checking his aim.

"Hey, the world may come to you, but you don't have to answer to it." He swept her hand into his, holding it tight. "No rules at Palazzo D'Inverno. You don't have to do anything you don't want to."

"Thanks." It was therapeutic to have someone validate her choices.

He pulled her to the couch and settled them both into it comfortably. The sun was low enough in the sky to cast a glow over the whitewashed building opposite the palazzo.

His fingers tangled in her hair, and she experienced the deepest sense of harmony she'd experienced in a long while. Maybe the deepest ever.

"You drove an Escalade?" she asked in a blatant attempt to change the subject. "Really?"

It seemed too domestic for a guy who liked to throw rules out the window.

Matt chuckled. "Yeah. But I sold it, along with everything else. Seemed easier, since I had no idea where I was going or when I was coming back. Sometimes it feels like that part of my life was a dream, and I have a hard time remembering who that guy was."

So he hadn't really fit into that suburban existence. Venice was more his speed, and he'd obviously taken to the laid-back lifestyle. She wondered if she would have given him a second glance if they'd met at a party in the States.

"Did you end up in Venice because it reminds you of your wife? You said you bought this palazzo for her."

The fingers in her hair stilled. "Amber. Yeah, I did buy it for her. But she died not too long after we got married. She never got the chance to visit."

"That's a shame."

His wife had never seen this beautiful place Matt had

given her. But Evangeline couldn't quite squelch the thrill of knowing she was the only woman who had slept in Matt's bed, who had lain with him on this couch and eaten at his table.

"The lack of ghosts is the most attractive thing about Palazzo D'Inverno. You know what that means in English? Winter Palace. Seemed appropriate to come here. My soul felt pretty frozen."

Her heart ached for him. He wandered in search of a cure for his grief. Maybe he'd found one—her.

Silly. Probably a recipe for disaster to imagine herself a healer. But the notion was still there, pinging around inside her.

"The Italian who built this palazzo called it that because he came here during the winter from someplace colder. So did you."

"True." The expression on his face caught her right in her aching heart. "But it's only warmer because you're in it. I wouldn't have come to Venice if Amber had stayed here. I sold the house in Dallas we'd bought together. I can't be around things with memories. I get too attached."

Of course he did. Anyone with Matt's depth would be shattered by the loss of someone he'd obviously loved. He and his wife had shared a house and a life and a level of commitment she couldn't comprehend.

He was staring out the window blindly when she glanced at him. "Is it hard to talk about her?"

"Yeah." He didn't elaborate, and the hard set of his mouth said he wasn't going to.

For a guy who had easily told stories at lunch about his college days, closing off must mean it was a very taboo subject. She had an extra store of mercy for that kind of pain, especially for someone who'd been so very nice about Franco's invasion.

Maybe she'd stayed in the worst sort of foolish gamble—

betting that Matt wouldn't hurt her because he empathized with her pain.

Through the glass, she watched a bird pecking at the marble balcony. "When I was in an interview and the reporter asked a question I didn't want to answer, I'd use a code word. My manager would smoothly and quickly rescue me. We'll have one, too. Whenever one of us touches on a sensitive subject, the code word is sacred. It means 'get me out of this. No more questions.'"

That melted the stone from his expression. "What kind of code word?"

"You pick. Make it silly. That way, we can lighten the mood at the same time."

"Armadillo," he suggested immediately. "They walk funny."

The way he said it, all serious about the assignment, made her giggle. "See? It works. So do you want to call *armadillo* about Amber?"

His mouth twitched. "Maybe. And maybe I'm starting to get through it. I can say her name out loud without flinching. Progress."

Because of her? Maybe she hadn't given herself enough credit in the healing department.

Then he tipped up her chin and pierced her with those pale blue eyes. "I'll be your manager. In the interview."

Her lungs seized. "What are you talking about? I'm not doing the interview."

He didn't get it at all. Had she lost her gamble already?

"But if you wanted to, I'd stay right there with you. Say the word and I'll rescue you." He smiled and it was so gentle, she almost smiled back. "Nothing wrong with both of us making progress."

So, he'd obviously drawn a few of his own conclusions about her reasons for saying no.

She shook her head. "I don't want to do the interview."

"Okay."

And like that, he dropped the subject in favor of launching into a discussion about what she might like for dinner. She responded, but most of her attention was back on Matt's offer to be with her during the interview.

If he'd pushed, her heels would have dug in. But he never forced her to explain herself—backing her into an emotional corner was the fastest way to irritate her. It was almost like he knew.

"Matt?" He didn't even comment about how she'd interrupted him. "You'd do that for me? Rescue me if I say *armadillo?*"

"Sure." His brows wrinkled in confusion as he squeezed her hand. "I said I would. Does that mean you're going to do the interview?"

Patiently, he waited her out, his silence nothing more than encouragement to go on if she chose. Or not, if she chose, which was usually the path she took. "I don't know. I've had a strict no-interviews policy since the surgery."

"Do you get stage fright in front of all those cameras or something? Just picture them in their underwear."

The mental image of cameras wearing a pink, lacy bra-and-panty set made her giggle. "That's not the problem. I just don't like the questions."

"Well, no offense, but that guy doesn't strike me as a hard-hitting news journalist. If he asks you about anything more strenuous than where you shop, I'll fall over in a dead shock." He brushed a thumb across her cheek. "If I was going to jump back in the water, I'd get my feet wet with a small-time Italian talk show first."

"I'll think about it."

She'd think of nothing but. Because his point was valid.

He gave her plenty of space by bounding up immediately to cook dinner. She trailed him to the kitchen to watch him beat the raw ingredients into submission, which she thoroughly enjoyed.

"While you're sitting there," Matt said as he pulled covered platters from the refrigerator. "You should start thinking of the proper way to thank me for this fantastic dinner."

She returned his wicked grin. "Exactly how good of a cook are you?"

"My mama taught me well. Though I believe she intended for me to feed myself. Not use my culinary skills to seduce women."

"But you're so good at both. She should be proud."

They laughed and traded banter, and dinner was everything she'd anticipated when he'd asked her to stay—a low-key, enjoyable evening with a man who liked her.

Matt wasn't the only one who needed to heal. She got that. But he had a prayer of getting there one day, especially if she truly helped him along. Unfortunately, there wasn't anything he could do in return to fix her vocal cords. She was permanently scarred, and at best, this Venice interlude was a distraction from the rest of her life and what she would do with it.

For ten years, she'd worked hard, so hard, to climb the charts. Nothing had been handed to her. Only by tapping into her emotions and feeding her muse with the next greatest adventure had she found success. Being aimless and idle grated on her almost as much as having no voice. She wanted—needed—meaning again, but what if she invested in something and it kicked her to the curb like music had?

The public's hostile clamoring for a piece of her just increased the difficulty in answering the questions. But how long could she go on ignoring the fact that the person who really needed that answer was Evangeline?

Milano Sera was a benign compromise, and the addition of Matt's strength made it somehow seem a lot safer. She should do it, if for no other reason than to gain some progress toward the answers. If Franco put her back against the wall and demanded an explanation of who she was going to be from now on, all she had to do was say *armadillo*.

* * *

Evangeline's former publicist agreed to work with *Milano Sera*'s team to arrange an interview, with two important stipulations—Matt must be given free rein on the set, and Franco had to tape the show remotely from Vincenzo's house.

No one argued. Two days after Evangeline tucked her belongings into Matt's dresser, the taping was a go.

She checked her makeup one last time in the framed mirror above the marble double-sink vanity. A remote taping meant limited resources, so she'd handled her own clothes and hair in the ensuite bathroom she'd been sharing with Matt. No change from regular life; the days of stylists and three dedicated makeup artists were long over. She didn't mind. The activity gave her a chance to calm her nerves.

Eva stared back at her from the mirror. Whatever happened today was happening to Eva. She had to remember that.

When she and Matt entered Vincenzo's palazzo, the buzz of activity stopped as if a plug had been pulled. A statuesque, authoritative woman in her forties barreled over to pump Evangeline's hand and escort her to the makeshift set, introducing herself as the show's producer.

Gingerly, Evangeline perched in the tall, canvas chair the producer had indicated and smoothed her fuchsia skirt as the camera director lined up the shot, fiddled with the lighting and barked orders at the stressed assistants. Matt watched it all without comment from the edge of the camera zone, one hand shoved in his back pocket. It was a deceptively casual stance, but his keen blue eyes missed nothing.

So far, so good. The anchor of Matt's presence went a long way.

Franco strolled over to take the other chair, appropriately slick in his Armani suit and practiced smile.

"Eva, I'm happy you changed your mind."

Sure he was. The ratings boost would likely make his year.

An assistant clipped the small microphone inside Evangeline's strappy top, which she'd specifically chosen because its design allowed for the microphone to be completely hidden.

"I enjoy watching *Milano Sera* so I'm happy to be here, as well."

Franco nodded, though he surely didn't believe either falsehood. Another assistant dashed over and frowned over Evangeline's microphone as Franco murmured to the statuesque director.

"There's a small difficulty, *signorina*." The assistant unclipped the microphone and dashed away to return with another one. "Speak to Franco now."

"Thank you for having me, Mr. Buonotti," she said obediently.

Franco shook his head and tapped his earpiece. "It's no good."

The producer and another man whispered to each other furiously as assistants milled around.

"What's the problem?" she asked Franco. Foreboding settled in her chest at his blank expression.

"Your voice, *cara*. It's not working well with this remote equipment," he explained, not the least bit apologetic, as if the equipment wasn't to blame, but *she* was. "Too low. They can't get it to register."

Her cheeks heated. Rejected by the taping equipment.

"Try again. Speak directly into the microphone." Franco cleared his throat. "Tell me, Eva. What is your life like now that your voice has been so tragically altered?"

A cold, clammy sweat broke out across her neck. Slicked her palms. Eva. He was talking about Eva's voice. Not hers.

"Um." She shook her head as her brain shut down.

Matt was wrong. The interview hadn't even started yet, and already Franco was probing her wounds with inflammatory phrasing. Fashion tips, she could handle. Why had she naively believed Matt that shopping would be Franco's focus?

Armadillo.

Her throat clamped closed and she couldn't get the word out. Couldn't make any sound at all.

This wasn't happening to Eva, it was happening to *her.*

But then Matt was there, leading her from the chair and tersely informing the producer that Eva did not deign to give interviews to second-rate talk shows without proper equipment.

"Nice," she said when she could speak again, which happened right around the time she crossed the threshold of Matt's house. "You're the best manager I've ever had."

"I'm sorry I suggested that."

He was still bristling, his expression hard and unyielding. And maybe a little frightening.

"It's not your fault."

"It is. I had no idea he'd be so insensitive."

He muttered a particularly inventive slur on Franco's paternity and heritage simultaneously.

Amazing how Matt could still make her smile in the midst of emotional uproar.

"If it makes you feel better, you made up for it, like by quadruple."

It hadn't been merely a rescue, but an expert extraction completed without letting on to her distress *and* giving *Milano Sera*'s team the impression they'd upset her diva personality. A miraculous feat in her opinion.

"It does not make me feel better." He flipped on the lights to dispel the February gloom. Instantly, she cheered. This *was* still a haven. "You told me exactly what would happen. But I was so sure I knew what would help."

Clearly frustrated, he heaved a sigh.

She tucked herself into his embrace and laid her head on his shoulder, right at the hollow she'd first discovered while they were dancing. "You've given me exactly what I needed. A place to block all that out."

His arms tightened, drawing her into his body deliciously. "I'm glad, sweetheart. Palazzo D'Inverno is available to you as long as you want it."

Not the house. You.

He helped, in so many intangible ways. In his arms, nothing seemed as bad.

She didn't say it.

If nothing else, Franco had shown her the protection Eva had provided in the past had all but vanished. She had nothing left to be rejected but the deepest part of herself, and that was something she refused to risk.

No matter how much she wished Matt held some sort of magic key to her future, he couldn't be anything more than a brief distraction. There was no question their Venice affair was going to be hot, fantastic…and short-lived.

She refused to become dependent on a man—not just a man, but one with his own demons—to fill the gap music had left behind, and she could see it happening as if Matt's beautiful eyes had turned into a crystal ball. Worse, it would be all take and no give, because her store of trust was in short supply. That was totally unfair.

How much longer did it really make sense for her to stay?

Seven

Matthew blinked and it was somehow Saturday already.

Evangeline filled his house, exactly as he'd envisioned, and blinded him to everything else. They didn't go out, more through his insistence than hers. He'd set up an account at both the local pharmacy and the grocery store so Evangeline could order whatever she needed to be delivered. The creative thank-you she'd given him for his thoughtfulness still ranked as one of the highlights of the week.

And there had been a lot of highlights, especially the gradual lightening of the shadows in her eyes, which he'd only made worse with his meddling. He was gratified she'd stayed long enough to let him undo the hurt he'd caused.

He'd never had a relationship with no promises past breakfast. Certainly never thought he'd have suggested it. Every morning, he expected—braced—to find she'd left in the middle of the night.

It was getting old. But the terms were too necessary to change.

The wanderlust in her eyes was unmistakable. When she talked about performing in Budapest or Moscow, her expression reminded him of when he was inside her. Rapturous.

She couldn't sing, but she still liked roaming. Eventually, she'd move on and leave him behind.

Which was good. This thing between them was amazing, but he couldn't keep it up, not long term.

He glanced at his phone. With the time difference, Mama should be at one of her Saturday-morning fundraisers right about now. The perfect time to call. He dialed and waited for voice mail to pick up.

"You've reached Fran Wheeler. I'm busy saving the world with style and grace. Leave a message."

His mother's voice poured alcohol on the exposed wound of guilt in his gut, which was approximately half the size of Texas. "It's me, Mama. Just checking in to let you know I'm still alive. Talk to you later."

He wouldn't, because he never called when she might actually answer.

What would he say? *Sorry about taking off. No, still not coming home. Still not capable of being the Wheeler you raised me to be.*

He had to go home and pick up his responsibilities with Wheeler Family Partners.

But he'd left because he couldn't do it any longer, couldn't see his grandfather's empty desk every day. Couldn't attend fundraisers and ribbon cuttings without Amber. Couldn't watch Lucas and Cia sneak off during the boring parts of events and return with all that love and affection dripping from their faces.

It was too hard.

So he'd live in the present and wring every bit of pleasure out of it.

He sat at the kitchen island and watched Evangeline wash lunch dishes in the sink. He cooked and she washed dishes. Worked for him—the view was very enjoyable from his stool.

"What do you want to do now?" he asked. She flashed

a naughty smile over her shoulder. "Twice this morning wasn't enough for you?"

"Never enough. I like you too much."

Yeah. He liked her, too. Everything was fun. Showers. Dishes. Long talks in the afternoon. "The weather is supposed to be unseasonably warm today. What if we have dinner on the roof?"

"There's a rooftop patio?" Her gravelly voice was hopeful as she dried the last dish and put it away.

That voice. It still dug in, sharp and hot inside no matter how many times he heard it. It was the first thing he wanted to hear in the morning and the last thing he wanted to hear before he went to sleep.

"Did I forget to mention that?"

"Never mind dinner. Show it to me right now."

"Sure." He took her hand and led her outside.

The breeze from the canal was chilly, but bearable, as they climbed the outside stairs to the roof. Venice unfolded as they walked out onto the patio.

Evangeline gasped. "Oh, Matt. I could live here. Right here in this spot. The view is amazing."

"I know. It's one of the reasons I bought this palazzo."

Several of the plants lined up in clay planters against the railing had withered and died, but a few remained green, fresh against the backdrop of browns, terra-cotta and white from the surrounding buildings.

Millions of dollars of real estate stretched on either side of the canal. Once, he'd have taken in the structures with a critical eye, evaluated the resale value, calculated the square footage. Mapped the location and noted the neighborhood features automatically.

None of that could compare to the gorgeous vision standing next to him. The look on her face—he'd move a mountain with a teaspoon if it put that expression of awe and appreciation there.

"You can see the spires of San Marco. And Santa Maria

della Salute. Isn't it beautiful?" She pointed, but he was busy looking at her. Her loose curls blew against her cheek and her eyes were luminous and his gut tightened. His reaction to her was so physical, so elemental. Would he ever get tired of that?

"Yeah. Beautiful." His fingers ached to sink into her hair. Among other things.

That was the beauty of their arrangement. They did whatever they wanted, when they wanted to do it. And he wanted her, wanted to make her feel as good as she made him feel. Right now.

"Let's go back inside."

"What? Why?" She flicked him a puzzled glance and turned her attention back to Venice.

"Because," he said hoarsely, and the unexpected catch in his throat swallowed the rest of the words.

With obvious concern, she eyed him. "Are you okay?"

No. Not hardly. He tugged on her hand. "Come back downstairs. Please. I want to be with you."

"You *are* with me." Her gaze traveled over him. Finally, she caught on to his urgency and grinned. Wickedly. "Oh. Well, I've got news for you. My girl parts work the same whether I'm inside or outside."

Attention firmly on him, she leaned in and teased him with a butterfly kiss while her hands wandered underneath his shirt. He was already half-aroused, and her fiery touch drained heat south instantly.

"Evangeline." He groaned as her fingers dipped into the waistband of his jeans to cup his bare butt. "We're on the roof."

"Uh-huh," she murmured against his mouth. "If you want me, take me, cowboy."

The kiss turned carnal as her tongue crashed with his and they drank from each other. She stole his reason, transformed his desire into crushing need, drew him out of time and place.

He was totally hooked on it.

Tilting her head, he changed the angle, went deeper, fed his senses with the feast of Evangeline.

Their hips aligned, seeking the heat, the promise of completion just beneath their clothes.

He nearly lost his balance as his shirt came over his head, gripped tight in her fists. She threw it to the concrete. Before he could protest, she had his zipper down and her warm hands stroked his flesh, coaxing him out from behind the fabric of his underwear.

They were on the roof. And he was on display.

Then she knelt. Her mouth closed over his length, and conscious thought escaped him as his knees weakened. Running on pure carnal instinct, he pushed deeper until the licks of fire spread through his blood like an inferno, tightening into a knot at his center. He couldn't keep from coming another second.

"Hold up, sweetheart."

He eased from her mouth and in a flash, dropped to the ground and pulled her into his lap. The breeze cooled his fevered skin. Street sounds wafted from below. And he didn't care. She encouraged him to do new things, things he'd never do under normal circumstances, and somehow it made sense.

In moments, her clothes landed in a heap and her mouth landed on his, legs wrapped around his waist, exactly the way he liked.

Yes. He fed the flames as he slid into her. Eyes closed, he froze, sustaining the perfect pleasure of being inside her sweet body, reveling in the physical, carnal hunger that drove him to join with her.

He'd left Dallas desperate to feel again. She'd burrowed underneath the ice-covered inertia and sensitized him. To the limit.

She moaned his name and rolled her hips, drawing him deeper than should have been possible. The roof, the air,

Evangeline—*something*—heightened the sensations, spiraling him toward oblivion faster, stronger, fiercer than ever before.

Her gaze captured his, and the morning sunlight refracted inside her eyes, brightening them. The ache of near release bled upward, into his chest, his throat.

Lids fluttering, she surrendered to an exceptionally strong climax. It rippled down his length and detonated his own release. The blast echoed in his head, blacking out his vision.

He held her slumped form, dragging oxygen into his lungs. That had been…different. And in a relationship full of different, how could there be so many shades yet undiscovered?

How could he crave still more when they'd delved so deeply already?

When she shifted, resettling in his lap, clarity blew away the awe of the moment.

"Evangeline. We forgot to use a condom."

"It's okay," she mumbled against his shoulder. "It's the wrong time of the month."

Women and their bodies—that was a mystery he'd yet to solve even after being with Amber for years. He heaved out a shudder of a breath.

"Sure?"

"Well, either way, too late now." She smiled up at him. "And it was worth it. I don't know how you do that to me. It was unbelievable. Even for us."

"Yeah. It was."

She'd noticed the difference too, but attributed it to the lack of a barrier. Which he didn't believe for a second. Sure the sensation was mind-altering. He'd do it again in a heartbeat if given a safe opportunity. But there was more to it than forgetting a condom, and he feared it had everything to do with Evangeline. With who he was around her. Because of her.

"We'll be extra careful from now on." She wagged her finger at him. "You have to stop being so adorable and sexy."

"Me?" That he could never get used to. It was disturbing when she told him how much he turned her on, which she did frequently. Disturbing because he liked it, and didn't understand what about her was so compelling, when she and Amber were such polar opposites. "You're the one who was all gorgeous with the hair in your face."

"You've got it bad and you might as well admit it."

His pulse stuttered. "Got what bad?"

A crush? Feelings? Was she staring down the barrel of their relationship and seeing things that weren't there?

Or was he making excuses for things he didn't want to examine too closely?

"An addiction to inventive positions," she explained with a wicked laugh. "And locations, apparently."

His muscles relaxed, and he eased her up to help her get dressed, then stepped into his own clothes. "That's all you, honey. I'm just here for the food."

Her laugh uncurled across his skin with gravelly teeth and stayed there. She affected him in so many ways. And not all of them were good.

A dose of guilt wormed into his consciousness. He'd found a temporary cure for his ills, but how fair was it to keep using Evangeline?

"Hey." He caught her hand and brought it to his lips. "You know I don't have much to offer. Emotionally. Right?"

She nodded, gaze searching his quizzically. "I'm not confused about what's going on between us. We're keeping the demons at bay until it doesn't work any longer. Were *you* confused?"

"No. Just checking."

Keeping the demons at bay. Yeah, that was exactly what they were doing. She knew he wasn't capable of anything more right now.

They meandered downstairs to do absolutely nothing except be together.

It shouldn't have been so easy. They should get on each other's nerves. Or complain about socks on the floor, dishes in the sink. Argue about something.

They didn't.

The longer he spent in Evangeline's company, the less he recognized himself. He hadn't put on a suit since the masked ball; he hadn't ironed a shirt or balanced his checkbook. T-shirts and spending money recklessly felt far too comfortable. As comfortable as Evangeline.

He hadn't dwelled on Amber in days. Wasn't that the point of all this? Why did it feel so strange?

Venice provided a much-needed break from real life as he searched for a way to get back to Dallas, to the responsible, centered, married man he'd been. When he'd understood his place in the world and woke up happy every morning.

He didn't know what would work to turn back time, or if what he sought existed. But he was starting to wonder—if he'd known what to look for, what would he have found instead of glittery, wrong-for-Matthew-Wheeler Evangeline?

And would he recognize it, now that Evangeline had so filled him he couldn't see around her?

Late one afternoon, Evangeline's phone buzzed. She retrieved it and flopped on the couch next to Matt, then glanced up from the text message to catch his gaze.

"Vincenzo's cousin, Nicola, is throwing a small dinner party," she said. "Tonight. Do you want to go? It's casual. He assures me the guest list is well vetted."

They hadn't left the house in a week. Self-preservation warred with the gypsy part of her soul that liked parties and people and experiences. All of her parts liked Matt, so it wasn't a hardship to wake up in his bed every morning.

"Sounds fun. As long as you're okay with it."

And that was why. He was amazing and intuitive and

never crowded her. Gradually, she'd stopped practicing her exit strategy and just enjoyed hanging out with him. Plus, she'd grown rather fond of starring in Matt's rodeo. The man shattered her with those eyes alone.

Was she okay with going out? It was dinner at Nicola's house, not a public flogging. She hesitated.

"Nicola lives on the other end of the Grand Canal. How should we get there?"

With silent, reassuring strength, he covered Evangeline's hand with his. "Private water taxi. Put on a big hat and a scarf. It'll be dark. No one will know it's you."

"Done." She accepted the invitation and deleted the other text message she'd received from her half sister, Lisa, without reading it, then spent an hour getting ready. Which gave her plenty of time to get worked up about her sister.

Lisa was seventeen. And her parents had been married. The anger, the sheer resentment was embedded deep. Their father had chosen a life with one daughter over the other—Evangeline would never forgive that. She sent Lisa extravagant Christmas gifts in a petty attempt to show her father there were no hard feelings. And maybe to quietly announce that hey, no dad needed for her to be a huge success.

Evangeline hadn't spoken to her sister since the botched surgery. How many texts did she have to ignore for Lisa to give up? It wasn't like they were real family.

Putting it out of her mind, she vowed not to let unpleasant history ruin the fun evening she and Matt had planned.

When Evangeline returned downstairs, Matt was waiting for her, dressed in dark jeans and a sweater. His eyebrows rose.

A floppy hat covered her pinned-up hair, a scarf hid the lower half of her face and giant sunglasses completed the disguise.

"Perfect." Matt shot her a playful grin. "Except maybe lose the glasses. It is nighttime."

She slipped them off and returned his smile. "Happy?"

"Always."

That thrilled her to no end, to be responsible for Matt's happiness. That was part of the reason she stayed. It was powerful to watch him slowly heal.

The taxi picked them up at Palazzo D'Inverno's water entrance and motored away from the dock. The driver steered under the Ponte dell'Accademia and up the canal to Vincenzo's cousin's house. Twinkling stars competed with the twinkle of Venice, both lit for the night with stunning brilliance.

They arrived a few minutes later. Once inside, Evangeline started to introduce Matt and realized with no small amount of mortification that she didn't know his last name. It hadn't seemed important, until now.

With a quick grin that said he'd read Evangeline's mind, he stuck out his hand to Nicola Mantovani, their hostess. "Matt Wheeler."

He repeated it to Nicola's boyfriend, Angelo. Vincenzo shook Matt's hand and introduced his lady friend for the evening, whose name Evangeline promptly forgot. He never called his dates again anyway.

Nicola lifted an unobtrusive finger toward a uniformed servant, who sprang forward to pass out wineglasses full of deep red Chianti. The tiny, dark-haired Italian raised her glass. "A toast. To new friends."

Expertly, Nicola finessed everyone to the lushly appointed salon where they took seats and chatted politely.

When Vincenzo launched into an impassioned review of the performance he'd seen at Teatro alla Scala the prior weekend, Evangeline leaned in to whisper in Matt's ear. "Wheeler. That's a nice last name."

Matt grinned. "We haven't formally introduced ourselves, have we?"

"Evangeline La Fleur." She stuck her hand out in mock solemnity. "Nice to meet you, Matt Wheeler."

Vincenzo paused long enough to drain his glass and motioned for a refill.

In the silence, Angelo asked Matt, "What do you do?"

"I'm a partner at a commercial real estate firm in Dallas, Texas."

No hesitation. No dodging the question. It was clearly how he defined himself or the answer wouldn't have come so quickly. It put an odd barb in her stomach because she wouldn't have been so quick with her own answer.

"Oh, do you know J. R. Ewing?" Angelo snickered at his own joke. Evangeline rolled her eyes, but Matt just laughed.

He was such a good guy to spend time with her friends and not call them out for being lame. But here she could relax and just be herself, without the pressure of Eva.

"Real estate." Nicola wrinkled her nose. "Houses?"

"No, we haven't delved into residential. We sell office buildings. Downtown high-rises." When he warmed to the subject, the pang in her stomach poked a little harder. He loved his job. It was all over his expression. "Land for development. That sort of thing."

We. Not *I.* An interesting choice of phrasing. Who was the *we?*

"High-rises. That sounds impressive." Nicola's nose unwrinkled and she leaned forward, suddenly a bit more interested in Evangeline's companion now that she scented money.

"Matt's very successful," Evangeline threw in, though she didn't know much about the ins and outs of the life he'd left behind. Neither last names nor pre-Venice activities had ranked very high on the priority list of their discussions. She'd always assumed it was by design, since Matt's wife was a taboo piece of that past.

But really, of course he was successful. Look at him.

He squeezed her hand. "Evangeline's being kind. I've been on an extended vacation. Wheeler Family Partners was the top-selling firm in Texas last year, but its current success is due to my brother. Not me."

"You work for a family business?" Nicola asked, and Matt nodded, explaining how the other partners were his dad and brother and the firm had been in his family for over a hundred years.

No one else seemed to notice the catch in his voice, but it sliced at her.

Family meant nothing to her, was almost a foreign word. But to Matt, it seemed as if it had been the cornerstone of his existence before Venice. He'd communicated far more than the simple logistics of a job—he'd belonged to a unit.

He wandered in search of answers now, but did he eventually want to return to his roots? She didn't want to ask. Didn't want it to matter. But the barb in her stomach was also due to realizing they were less alike than she'd assumed.

She waited until after dinner, when they'd settled into the water taxi to return to Matt's house, to bring it up again. "Tell me more about your life in Dallas."

With a laugh, he kissed her sweetly. "Why? Do you need to take a nap? That would be so boring you'd nod off in a second."

Her lips curved. "Boring? You? There's no way the guy who put his hand under my dress on a balcony could ever be boring."

"I drove a sports utility vehicle, Evangeline."

"But you left it all behind." His wife's death had turned him into a drifter. Like her. They'd both been honed by tragedy but had yet to recognize their new shape. She desperately wanted to feel that kinship with him again after learning they'd come from such different places. "So it doesn't matter now, right?"

"It matters. I walked away from a legacy. The name of the firm is Wheeler Family Partners. That pretty much encapsulates it. Family is everything. And I abandoned them." His voice never wavered as he listed his sins.

Strength. He had it in spades and it pulled at her. The men in her life were weak. Spineless. Matt regretted his actions but took full responsibility for what he'd done.

"I didn't mean to poke at scars. Armadillo?" she offered.

"Yeah. It's not a great subject." He curled her palm against his. "What was your life like when you were singing?"

"Busy. Lonely." The hand holding hers tightened. Encouraging her to go on. He was so easy to be with—maybe she could open up, just a little. "The guy from Vincenzo's party, Rory, he was supposed to be the cure for that. We were so similar, both with careers in the industry. Both happy being nomads. He had some bad habits, but I stepped over the empty Jack Daniel's bottles because I was in love with him. Turns out he wasn't content to be saddled with a has-been."

"I'm sorry."

"I'm not. Longevity isn't one of my gifts." She'd have tried, for Rory. And probably would have bungled it all up. "That's what made being an in-demand vocalist so great. I sang all over the world, was constantly on the move."

She'd loved it, loved having a new destination, new experiences.

And that was the gist of it, wasn't it? She and Matt had a kinship born of shared pain, but it was tenuous at best. A successful, solid real estate broker who valued family had nothing in common with a music business has-been who sported a giant albatross called Lack of a Career around her neck.

Besides, his heart still belonged to his wife, would always belong to his family. Hers had been cut from her chest by the same blade that destroyed her career. Maybe even before that.

She'd shared this time with Matt because they were both slaying their demons.

How much longer would it take for this refuge to crumble around her?

Eight

Evangeline rolled over and pulled the sheets up around her neck. Cold. And still dark. Though her brain languished in the fog of semiconsciousness, she could tell Matt wasn't asleep. His breathing was too even.

Two weeks and four days into it and she could already gauge his state of consciousness. She also knew his favorite foods, the exact rhythm to move her hips to make him explode, how to get that blinding, sincere smile out of him that shivered her insides.

And if he was awake, she knew she'd never go back to sleep.

They were becoming dangerously entangled for two ships who were supposed to be passing in the night.

Supposed to be. But she was still here.

She kept looking for a reason to leave. Kept waiting for claustrophobia to set in or for Matt's true colors to shine through. The longer she spent with him, the more convinced she became that he was the real deal and she could trust him. He was a genuine guy who wasn't looking for the quickest way to get rid of her. Who treated her like he'd stumbled upon a rare treasure.

Instead of scouting for the exit, she stayed. The longer she stayed, the more obstacles she saw to keeping this Venice bubble afloat.

Why couldn't she have met Matt in six months? A year? At any point in the future when she'd figured out who she was going to be and could give Matt what he deserved—someone a lot more together, at a different place in her life.

She scooted across the cool sheets and nestled into his arms. "You need a glass of warm milk?"

He kissed her temple. "Did I wake you up? Sorry."

"You didn't."

But maybe on some level, he had.

That instantaneous spiritual bond hadn't dimmed in the slightest. Sometimes, he finished her sentences, and sometimes, she didn't have to speak at all. It was more than gelling and she puzzled over the indescribable, powerful nature of their relationship.

It should feel weird. Suffocating. It didn't.

"I'll go downstairs so you can sleep."

Something was bothering him. Matt's ghosts continually haunted him and lots of great sex hadn't produced quite the exorcism she'd have wished.

She snaked an arm over his chest to hold him in place. "Don't you dare. Talk to me."

"It's not a middle-of-the-night subject. But thanks." His hand wandered over to stroke her breast and as lovely as that was, his touch carried a hint of preoccupation.

"Anything is a middle-of-the-night subject. It's dark. Sleepy. What better environment is there to lay it all out?" Unless he was about to call it off. That froze her pulse. She didn't want it to be over.

She'd thought they were both happy to live in the here and now. Both happy to see what unfolded. The lack of boundaries made it easier for her to stay but also made it easier—for either of them—to walk away.

Should she have checked in with him before now?

The hand on her breast stilled, but didn't move away. "You wouldn't rather go back to sleep?"

"I'd rather you weren't upset. Tell me, and let me make it all better. That's what I'm here for, right? To beat back the demons." Which was a two-way street, and he did his part well. "But unlike other forms of self-medication, I don't come with a hangover."

"You don't pull any punches, do you?" A deep breath lifted his chest. "I was thinking I should be over Amber by now."

"What? Why would you think *that*?"

Oh, that was such a better subject than calling it off. He hardly ever mentioned his wife, and she respected his privacy. But curiosity pricked at her, naturally. What had Amber been like? What was so special about her to have shattered Matt into so many pieces?

"It's been a year and a half. How can I still be so messed up?"

"You can't put a time frame to grief. Life doesn't have checklists."

"We weren't married a whole year. She's been dead longer than the length of our marriage."

"So? You loved her." Obviously a lot, more than Evangeline had ever loved anyone, or could even imagine. She could, however, *easily* imagine how it would feel to be the object of such unending devotion.

Especially Matt's.

That put a hitch in her lungs. She suddenly, unreasonably wished for something impossible—the hope that she might one day take Amber's place in his heart. Impossible, because she'd have to open herself up in return and trust Matt with her deepest layer. Impossible, because he was still hung up on his wife. That was the biggest obstacle of all.

Apparently dark-and-sleepy was a good environment for her conscience to spill confessions, as well. As long as she didn't start doing it out loud…

Matt shifted restlessly. "Am I doomed to suffer for the rest of my life because I fell in love with someone? It's not fair."

He was destroyed. No one should have to bear that much of a burden without relief.

"I don't have all the answers." She rested her palm on his heart, which beat strongly despite her suspicion it was badly broken. "The only thing I know for sure is life sucks and then it gets better until it gets worse again. Sometimes I think God likes to see what happens when the carpet is pulled out from under you."

After a long minute of silence, he said, "It doesn't bother you that I'm moping around over another woman?"

Well, now that you mention it...

"I didn't say that." Boy, he'd taken her no-subject-off-limits-in-the-middle-of-the-night seriously, hadn't he? Despite asking, she didn't think he'd actually appreciate knowing about the burning-in-the-gut jealousy of Amber she'd just discovered. "But we're cool. I understand. Of all people, trust me. I understand."

Probably too much. Other women wouldn't put up with being a form of self-medication. But Matt wasn't presenting her with a buffet of choices. What would she pick if he did?

The question bounced around inside her with no answer.

"The pastor at Amber's funeral said something that's stuck with me. The valleys of life are impartial and temporary. If that's true, I should get over it already, right?"

"Is *that* why you're beating yourself up? That's total crap!" Evangeline's vision grayed for a furious moment. Pastors should soothe people in their time of grief—not spew lies. "The valleys of life are anything but impartial. Or temporary. Both of us had the center of our existence ripped from our fingers. No warning. That's as personal as it gets, and I refuse to accept that we don't have the right to be pissed off about it because it's gone forever."

His arms tightened around her, holding her close, calming her. *He* was calming *her*. "Is that what happened? You had the center of your existence ripped away?"

"Yeah. I did." Her chin trembled.

"You don't talk about it."

Just like he didn't talk about Amber. "No voice. It kind of puts a crimp in the talking thing."

"That's a cop-out. Especially with me. Should I tell you again how sexy I think your voice is?"

She sighed. Transparency was one of the many things she couldn't avoid with Matt. It went hand in hand with the vibe between them. And it went both ways. He'd veered away from Amber on purpose, maybe to avoid talking about her. Or maybe to find some straw he could grasp from her own experiences. They were *both* fighting their way out of the valley.

He was so compassionate and decent and didn't want anything from her but her company. She should honor that.

"I lost everything." She shut her eyes. "Not just my career. I sang my whole life, from as early as I can remember. Back then, my voice was the one thing that belonged to me and no one else. Singing was a coping mechanism."

"What were you coping with?" he asked gently.

"You know, stuff. My home life." She hadn't thought about it in years. But that had been the genesis of using her voice to express all the things going on inside.

"My dad, he was a hockey player for Detroit. A seagull who swooped in, got my mom pregnant and never called her again. She tracked him down, got child support. She moved to the U.S. so he could know his daughter. Guess how many times I heard from him?"

"Evangeline…" Matt nearly pulled her on top of him in a fierce hug, lips buried in her hair.

"It's fine. I'm over it."

"I don't think so," he murmured and softened the contradiction with a light kiss. "You started to say you had family in Detroit. When we were dancing."

God, she had. How did he remember that? "He's not my family. He lost that chance. But, I…have a…sister."

"Are you and your sister close?"

Evangeline laughed but it came out broken. "She worships me. Not like in a million-screaming-fans way. Because she wants to sing."

Lisa texted her all the time asking for career advice. Evangeline still didn't know why she'd ever answered. No one had helped her. But before the surgery, she hadn't been able to stop herself from pathetically responding each and every time. Once, she flew Lisa and three friends to London for a concert for Lisa's fifteenth birthday. It was the last time she'd seen her sister.

After the surgery, Evangeline went into a hole and stopped responding to the texts. One of these days, Lisa's name on her caller-ID wasn't going to cause such deep-seated anguish. She hoped. It wasn't Lisa's fault their father was a bastard.

"Is she any good?" Matt asked.

She shrugged. "I've never heard her sing. Too busy, I guess."

"You've got time now," he pointed out quietly, but his words reverberated in her head like the boom of a cannon.

"Yeah. I should call her." She wouldn't. What would she say? They had no relationship, had only ever connected over their mutual interest in singing. Now they had nothing in common other than a few strands of DNA. "Armadillo."

She was done with midnight confessions. Lisa was a corner she couldn't stand being backed into.

"I should call my brother. I haven't talked to him in a month." Matt rolled away and she missed his warmth. Had she hurt his feelings?

A sick niggle in her stomach unearthed the realization that she'd set up the code word as a way for him get out of difficult subjects, but only she used it.

"Is a month a long time?" she asked.

"We saw each other every day. His office was next to mine. We went to the same college, played basketball with some guys once a week. And you know. He's my brother. It's my job to make sure he stays out of trouble."

"You miss him."

It wasn't a question. She could hear it in his voice and didn't have to ask if they were close. Could Evangeline have a similar relationship with Lisa if she tried harder?

No. Evangeline wasn't cut out for family relationships. Didn't want to be. It hurt too much.

"That was before. When Amber was alive. After, I drifted through everything, disengaging until everyone stopped trying. I kept thinking something would happen to snap me out of it. Then my grandfather died and I realized. *I* had to snap me out of it. So I dumped my entire life in Lucas's lap and left." He chuckled derisively. "I even sold him my house. He's in *my* house with a wife he's gaga over, making new memories, about to deliver my parents their first grandchild. I should be there, living that life."

There. Not here. Venice was a temporary fix. She knew that. So why did it make her so sad?

"Are you jealous that your brother is happy?"

At least they had that in common.

"No. Not really. Maybe a little." He sounded defeated all at once. "Mostly I'm glad. I never thought he'd get married. He was kind of a screwup. But he met this woman who transformed him into a guy I didn't recognize. He's responsible. Committed. Expecting a baby who will be the first of the next generation of Wheelers. That was my role. A role I couldn't do any longer. And I need to figure out how to do it again."

He had more demons than she'd realized. "You're not just trying to get over Amber. You're trying to fit back into the life you had with her."

A life that included lineages. Babies. Roots and new

branches on the family tree. Concepts so alien she barely knew how to label them.

He huffed out a breath. "I can't. I know that. But for as long as I can remember, I've done the right thing. I ran Wheeler Family Partners, and I was good at selling real estate. Successful. Amber was a part of that. She had connections, came from a distinguished family. There were five hundred guests at our wedding. CEOs of Fortune 500 companies. A former U.S. president. The governor. We were happy being a power couple. People could depend on me. I want that back."

Her stomach dropped. No wonder he hadn't cared about her celebrity status or her money. He had his own social clout, in a world far removed from hers.

A cleft, one she hadn't realized was there, widened.

He hadn't embraced the wanderlust—he'd been desperate to find the magic formula for curing his grief so he could pick up the broken pieces of a life he'd abandoned, but yearned to return to.

Unlike her, he *could* go back. And would. Not only did neither of them have a whole heart to give to anyone else, they came from different places and were going different places.

She kissed his cheek. "I depend on you. Right now, you're my entire world."

How pathetic did that sound? He had a career waiting for him. A family. Both would welcome him back with open arms, she had no doubt. No mother who took the time to teach her son to cook would turn her back on him.

"Right now, I'm pretty happy being your entire world."

Shock flashed behind her rib cage. "Really? I thought you were heading toward the big breakup."

He *should* be heading toward the breakup. She should, too.

"What, you mean of us?" He laughed and shifted suddenly, rolling her against him, tight. "You're the best thing that's happened to me in a long time. Why would I give that up?"

"Isn't that what we've been talking about? You want to go home." Home to a place she couldn't follow. Her gypsy soul would wither and die in the suburbs. "This is…our Venice bubble. It's not going to last."

Quiet settled over them, and she waited for him to agree.

But he said, "I don't know if I *can* go home. My family— the obligations. It feels so oppressive. Like it's too much for me to handle. I want to be me again, but at the same time I want to keep hiding." He chuckled darkly. "God Almighty, I sound like the biggest pansy."

No, he sounded like a man in incredible turmoil. For once, she'd stayed. She'd done it as an attempt to block out the future, but instead, quite by accident, she'd discovered this sensitive, wonderful person. What a juxtaposition. She ached to salve his wounds, knowing the moment she did, he'd leave her.

Rock. Hard place.

"I want to sing. I can't. We're both stuck in a rut we can't get out of."

Matthew listened to the sound of Evangeline's heart against his and threaded fingers through her hair.

"Rut. Valley. Same difference."

There was nothing quantifiable about the grieving process. It had stages, or so he'd read. But they weren't easily identifiable so he had no idea if he'd gone through them all, remained immobilized in one, or had stumbled his way back to the beginning to run through them a second time.

He'd been stuck in the valley for far too long. And he was sick of it.

Her lips grazed his throat and stayed there. They'd both lost so much. Did she find it as comforting as he did to be in the arms of someone who understood? She not only understood, she'd given him permission to be mad.

That was powerful.

Because he *was* mad. And felt guilty about being mad. Evangeline somehow made it okay to let all that out, let it flow, and the anger cleansed as it burned through his blood.

"I was part of something," he said. "In Dallas. Some sons rebel against the family business, but I couldn't wait to be on the team. My parents were proud of me, and I thrived on that. Thrived on being married and looked forward to starting a family. Then it was gone and I couldn't function. I don't know how to get that back."

The sheer pressure of life without Amber had nearly suffocated him. But it was more than missing her. They'd been like cogs in a complex machine, complementing each other. He didn't know how to be successful without her.

"I admire you," she said quietly.

He snorted. "For what, disappointing everyone?"

That was at least half his onus—how did he face everyone again, knowing he'd abandoned them? Knowing they were eyeing him with apprehension, waiting for him to freak out again?

"For recognizing that you needed time away to get your head on straight. It was brave."

"Cowardly, you mean," he corrected. "People deal with pressure gracefully all the time. I cracked. It wasn't pretty."

"But you changed things. You left your comfort zone and struck out to fix it, without any idea how or where that would occur. That's sheer courage in my book."

He started to tell her she should reread that book but closed his mouth. She saw him differently. But that didn't mean she needed glasses. Perhaps he did.

"Thanks. That's nice to hear."

"You had a choice and made it." The unspoken *I didn't* wrenched his heart.

"Have you ever noticed the stuff people say when you're grieving makes no sense?" That was another gripe he'd been carrying around since the funeral.

"What like, 'Sorry for your loss'?"

"Yeah. My favorite is, 'But think of all you do have.'" He struggled to voice the anxiety whipping through him. Struggled to phrase it in a way that didn't sound self-centered. And gave up. This was Evangeline. He didn't have to pull punches. "It's meaningless. Thanks for pointing out I still have a mom and a dad. That makes it *all* better. And oh, yeah, I have my health. The fact that I'm still breathing is supposed to get me through the valley?"

"I got an, 'At least you still have all the money'. Don't get me wrong. I'm grateful I can afford to eat. A lot of people can't after losing their job. But money doesn't make up for losing who you were."

"Exactly." It was like she peered down his throat and read the words in his heart, expressing for him what he couldn't formulate. "Singing was your purpose. So what do you do now that it's gone, right?"

She laughed without humor. "Isn't that the million-dollar question?"

He'd meant it rhetorically, but something in her tone tugged at him. "Is it?"

She didn't answer, and he lightly bumped her head with his chest. "Middle-of-the-night. Nothing is sacred."

Don't call armadillo. His senses tingled. This was critically important, he could tell.

Her soft sigh drifted across his skin. "I don't know what to do now. That's my demon."

"The one I'm here to beat back for you?" The phantoms in her eyes weren't just from losing her voice. How could he have missed that? Because he'd been wallowing around in his own problems instead of tending to hers.

"Singing is all I'm good at. My only talent."

"Not hardly."

"Being good in bed isn't a talent." The eye-roll came through loud and clear.

He bit back a chuckle and the accompanying comment—
it is the way you do it.

"You're good at making me cheerful. That's something
no one else could accomplish, so don't knock it. But I was
going to say the music industry can't be easy to crack or
everyone would do it. Persistence is a talent. You worked
hard to achieve success."

"Yeah. Hard work." Her voice fractured. "There was a
lot of that."

There was more, something else she wasn't saying, and
she was hurting. The inability to fix it crawled around in
his chest. But this middle-of-the-night was exactly what
he'd asked for—the exploration of what two damaged souls
could become to each other.

Dang it if he'd fail at being what she needed.

"Hey." He brought her hand to his cheek and held it there,
reminding them both he wasn't going anywhere. "This
demon of yours, what does he look like? Big and scary?
Small and quick with a sharp stick? I'll do a much better job
of keeping him away if I have an idea what I'm looking for."

She laughed, low and easy, drawing a smile from him.
"Big. With claws. And he doesn't shut up. Ever."

"What does he sound like? James Earl Jones or more
Al Pacino?"

"Dan Rather."

Ah. "So your demon moonlights as a reporter who asks
you questions you don't like." And he'd bet the demon answered to the name *armadillo*.

"Yeah."

The single syllable quaked through her damaged vocal
cords and snapped something behind his rib cage.

"Like what?" he whispered, his voice nearly as raw as
hers.

"It's not the questions." She shifted and wet pooled into
the hollow of his shoulder right about where her eye had
been. Tears. "It's the lack of answers. Bad stuff happens.

They were just vocal cords. Why don't I know what to do next?"

"Because," he countered fiercely. "You're not out of the valley yet. Once you clear it, then you'll see where to go."

He had to believe that was true, had to believe it was possible. He wanted out of that valley—for himself, but also to show her the way.

"Music was a part of my soul." More tears dripped onto his chest, but he didn't wipe them away. Didn't move at all for fear of stemming the tide of her grief. "And I thought it always would be or I wouldn't have inked eighth notes on my body permanently. How do you find a new direction when something so ingrained is gone?"

Silently, he held her, suddenly furious that he didn't have the answers. Her anguish vibrated through him and wedged into a place he'd thought was dead and buried.

"I could have the tattoo removed," she continued brokenly. "Turned into something else. But what? Who am I going to be for the rest of my life?"

Yes. *That* was the million-dollar question. Evangeline voiced things he could hardly define, let alone articulate. They gelled because she struggled in exactly the same ways he did.

And perhaps they'd solve it together.

"Is there no way to keep a hand in music? Do you play an instrument?"

"Piano." She sniffed. "I wrote all my songs."

An odd sense of pride filled him with the admission. She'd produced something from nothing, using a creative energy he couldn't fathom.

"That's amazing. I thought other people wrote songs for recording artists."

A tune filled his head instantly. Hers. She'd written the notes, sang them. He wished he could have heard her live. Wished he could ask her to sing for him, here in the dark.

His gut split in two over the loss of something he'd never dreamed he'd want.

"Other people do write songs, when the artist is just a voice. Like Sara Lear." She growled. "I hate how catty that sounds. But geez, I could trip and fall into a piano and accidentally write a better song than the ones she sings."

Was her ability to connect dots broken or was she too close to see the obvious? "Then do it. Write one for her."

She shook her head against his shoulder. "I can't."

"Can't, or don't want to?" he countered softly.

"The words…they've all dried up."

"They'll come. You're an artist who isn't just a voice." He stroked her hair. "You'll figure it out. We'll both figure it out, and in the meantime, we'll hold each other in the dark and lay it all out there."

"Matt?" More snuffling. "I'm glad I stayed. I don't stay as a rule. No rules is nice for once."

Finally, he breathed a little easier. The conversation could have veered into something ugly. But he'd navigated it pretty well—he hoped—despite a distinct lack of experience with damaged souls, his or anyone else's. His relationship with Amber had been straightforward and undemanding. Safe.

He'd certainly never experienced quite so many highs and lows when she'd been alive.

"It can't last. This thing between us," he clarified. Evangeline was merely passing time with him until she figured out her next steps. She'd said as much. It shouldn't hollow him out—wasn't that what they were *both* doing here?

"I know that," he added, "but I can't stand to be in the valley alone. Please don't think less of me for selfishly dragging it out."

"I don't think you're selfish."

She wouldn't. Evangeline was the single most nonjudgmental person he'd come across. He could tell her anything. Had told her things he'd never said out loud. He didn't worry about disappointing her with his failures. Ironically, because he'd set out to be someone else with her, his internal censor-switch had shut off. He had the freedom to pour out the angst and fear he'd carried for months.

He wished he had more to give her in return and was suddenly sorry they'd met while they were both still stuck in the valley.

Nine

"Let's go out," Evangeline announced late one afternoon as they watched a movie, snuggled together on the couch.

Convinced he'd misheard, Matthew hit the volume, almost dropping the remote. "Out? As in out in public?"

Other than an occasional rooftop visit, they hadn't crossed the threshold of Palazzo D'Inverno since the dinner party a couple of weeks ago. He was on a first name basis with the grocery store delivery guy, who delighted in correcting Matthew's poor Italian.

"Yeah." She shrugged. "Take me on a date tonight."

"You hate dating."

"But I like you." She fluttered her lashes, coquettishly. "So I'm willing to make sacrifices. I might even let you talk my clothes off after."

"What's going on? Cabin fever?"

It was certainly starting to get to him. As much fun as Evangeline was—and really, was there such a thing as too much sex?—a slight sense of restlessness wouldn't go away, no matter what he did.

"I don't know. Maybe. I haven't worn makeup in for-

ever. I'd like you to see me in something other than one of
your T-shirts."

"I like you in my T-shirts. I like you best in nothing at
all," he threw in. "But I could go for some dinner with a
beautiful woman."

"Dinner and maybe a show." She leaped off the couch,
suddenly animated. "Ooh, I have the perfect dress. I haven't
worn it yet. I'm going to hog the bathroom. Do you need
anything out of it?"

"Nah." He grinned at her enthusiasm and flipped the
channel to a cable news station since the movie clearly
wasn't of interest any longer. "I'll be here. Waiting. For a
long time, I suspect."

An hour later, he'd donned a button-up shirt and ironed
some pants, the most effort he'd expended to get dressed in
ages. Evangeline still hadn't emerged from the bathroom
so he flopped on the couch to amuse himself by flipping
through the channels.

She called his name from the stairs.

He glanced at her and his heart locked up.

Evangeline La Fleur had put on yet another mask. She'd
transformed into a fantastical vision in a clingy blue dress,
honey-brown curls loose around her shoulders, sultry eyes
full of mystery and promise, legs shaped by spiked heels
that made his mouth water. And he'd kissed every inch of
that gorgeous body.

How could she still punch him so hard without a word
when they had few secrets between them any longer?

A button-up and kakis were far too casual to have *that*
on his arm. Actually, the man in the clothes left a lot to be
desired, as well. The glittery superstar walking down his
stairs had nothing in common with Matthew Wheeler.

"Ready?" she asked, her gravelly voice raw and thrill-
ing. Like always. It jump-started his lungs again as he stood
to meet her. She was still the same person underneath the
mask.

"I'm not sure. I think you've stolen my ability to walk. You're…I don't know what to call you. *Beautiful* is too simple a word. You're exquisite." Flustered, he straightened his belt and smoothed his hair. "Sure you want to be seen with me?"

She laughed, throatily, with her head thrown back. It was genuine and elemental, and he hardened in an instant.

"I'll ask you that same question in a little while, when we've drawn a lot of unwanted attention. I thought about playing it down, trying to blend. But it would be pointless. Anyway, I wanted to look nice. For you."

"For me?" That pleased him, enormously, and he yanked her into his arms, careful not to muss this gorgeous creature. "Thanks. It is a pretty good hit for my ego. And I will thoroughly enjoy looking at you all evening as I imagine what I'll say to talk your clothes off."

Her fingers walked down his chest and dipped into his pants to lightly graze his swollen flesh. "It'll have to be good. Maybe with some begging."

He groaned. "We're not going to make it out the door if you keep that up."

Withdrawing her hand, she smiled with a mischievous curve to her lips. "I'll save it for later then."

Eyes still crossed, he helped her into a coat and slipped on his own. Lacing their fingers, he led her outside into the night. Carnevale was long over and the cool March air held a hint of the Italian spring to come.

"Walk or water taxi?" he asked. "I thought we'd go to this little out-of-the-way place I found, instead of somewhere trendy. I hope that's okay. It's only a few blocks."

"Walk. I haven't seen nearly enough of Venice. There's a different feel when you're on the street, in the middle of it all. The view from your living room, or the roof even, is amazing. But removed. You know?"

Yes, he did. He'd been removed from everything for so long. Tonight, he was fully in the land of the living, with

Evangeline, and it did feel different. As if he'd emerged from a dark tunnel and the world had burst open around him.

As they strolled, other couples nodded or called *"Ciao"* upon passing. Streetside shops blazed with light behind glass, wares on display in the window. The pace of life in Venice ebbed and flowed with the canal waters, tranquil and slowed. Peaceful. History—the heartbreak, the triumphs— radiated from the very cobblestones and dripped from the stucco veneer of the ancient buildings.

People had lived and died in this city for centuries before Matthew's Northern European ancestors had jumped the pond to America. Life would continue on after Matthew was long gone. It was the here and now that counted.

He squeezed Evangeline's hand, and she glanced over at him through those soft brown eyes that he liked waking up to every morning. Not for the first time, he wondered if there was a way to stop dragging this thing out and do something crazy, like put a stake in the ground and hash out a plan to make it work long term.

Except he'd been searching for a way to move on after Amber's death, never realizing a step in that process might include falling in love with someone new.

It felt disloyal to Amber to think something like that.

This thing couldn't last. Not because he and Evangeline wouldn't work in real life. That was true, but surface level. Deep down, he wasn't sure he could do it again, give his whole being to someone else. Love someone else. Have a household, a baby, a life with someone else.

He'd created the temporary nature of his relationship with Evangeline to make her more comfortable with staying, but it was really an excuse. He'd latched onto it to avoid the truth—he wasn't ready to move on.

They found the restaurant easily. The maître d' showed them to their table, and Matthew ordered a bottle of Chianti, which the efficient staff brought immediately.

"Well. Here we are." Evangeline raised her glass and they clinked rims. "Our first date."

In a manner of speaking. Seemed strange to be on a first date with a woman he'd made squirm under his tongue as he knelt before her in the shower that morning. "Guess we did things out of order."

"That's okay. I'm not big on tradition."

"Like marriage?" Why in the world had he picked that rock to kick? He already knew her stance on commitment.

She wrinkled her nose. "Well, doesn't seem like it works out for many people, does it?"

It had for his parents and grandparents. Seemed to work tremendously well for Lucas and Cia, what little of their relationship he'd been around to witness.

His own marriage had been perfect. With Amber, he'd done things in the exact right order. They'd gone to the opera for their first date. Amber had worn gloves and left them in his car. On purpose, he knew, so she'd have an excuse to call him. Which she had done, two days later.

After three dates, he kissed her and three months to the day, he surprised her with a suite at the Fairmont, where they'd made love for the first time, in a nice evening full of potential. That's when he'd known he would propose, but he held off until they'd been together over a year, then, for Christmas, he'd given Amber a white-gold Tiffany engagement ring that had belonged to his grandmother. Everything safely unfolded according to plan.

For all the good it had done him.

Voices from the front of the restaurant interrupted his musing. Evangeline's face froze as a couple of sharply dressed teenage boys argued with the maître d', pointing at her.

"Sorry, they followed us in here," she said. "They noticed me on the street, but I figured they'd move on."

"What are you apologizing for?"

"Because it's invasive. Or it will be." She pasted on a

smile as the waiter came up behind her to whisper in her ear. She nodded, and the teenagers rushed over to babble incoherently in a mixture of Italian and English, shoving pieces of paper at Evangeline for her to sign. One of the boys handed her a Sharpie and brazenly lifted his shirt. She scrawled "EVA" in flowery script across his pectoral muscle.

Really? Matthew looked away as something black and sharp flared deep inside. These kids had no sense of decorum whatsoever.

And he absolutely did not want to admit the pain in his stomach had to do with Evangeline's palm on the guy's chest. Jealousy. As if she belonged to Matthew and he had a right to expect he'd be the only man she touched.

Evangeline was a good sport through it all. She posed with the boys for at least a dozen pictures, hastily snapped on their phones by the beleaguered waiter. When she was "on," her otherworldliness intensified, sharpening her beauty but making her seem almost untouchable.

She hadn't put on a mask—but taken one off. Eva was an extension of her essence.

Finally, the teenagers drifted out the door, leaving a tense silence draped over them both.

"My fans mean a lot to me." She flicked her nail across the tines of her fork without looking at him. "The ones I still have anyway. But it can be a bit much for someone not used to it. I knew better. I shouldn't have asked you to take me out."

"It's okay." Her biggest concern had been inconveniencing him or upsetting him, but he got that her celebrity went part and parcel with the rest. He reached out to cover her hand. "It's a small price to pay. You're worth it."

Her eyes grew shiny. "Thanks. We're lucky they weren't reporters."

They ate dinner without any more interruptions. When they left the restaurant, bright flashes halted them in their tracks, and he got a glimpse of the reason for her earlier concerns.

Two media-hounds lounged a few feet away, easily identifiable by their professional cameras and lack of interest in capturing the Venetian splendor all around them. Their sharp gazes were on Evangeline as she stepped into Matthew's side, snugging up against his ribs closely. Too closely. Seeking what? Protection?

A prickle of warning went down his spine.

The men blocked their path, crowding them with their solid builds and flat eyes. Not guys who looked eager to be reasonable.

"Eva," the shorter one on the left—American—called out. "Mind if we ask you a few questions?"

Matthew was about to calmly suggest it would be in their best interests to let them pass. But Evangeline's sharp intake of breath tripped something in his blood.

"I mind," Matthew said, and stepped in front of Evangeline, shielding her from the men.

"Who are you?" The one on the right zeroed in on Matthew. "*You* got time for a few questions? I'll be sure to spell your name right."

"No comment," Evangeline said and earned both men's pointed attention.

"Is that what your voice sounds like now?" The short one whistled. Nastily. "Like a cement mixer with boulders inside. Can I tape it?"

She was trembling against Matthew's back as she pulled on his arm. "We'll go the long way home."

Home. Not to a show, which she'd chattered about endlessly during dinner. If the reporter had latched onto anything else except her voice, Matthew would have let it slide.

These two idiots weren't ruining their night out. "Back off. We're of no interest to you."

"You're with Eva, you're news, buddy." The taller one

snapped off a few photographs, blinding Matthew with the flash.

"You want to get that camera out of our faces before I do it for you?" Matthew blinked hard in an attempt to clear the white starburst from his retinas.

"Are you threatening me, pretty boy?"

"Obviously not well enough if you have to ask. So I'll be clearer." Matthew nodded to both men curtly, tamping down his fury. "Stop harassing us or you'll be examining the ceiling of an Italian jail cell shortly. Or the ceiling of a hospital room. Your choice."

The men glanced at each other, smiling cruelly. "You gonna take on both of us? Over *her*?"

Her. As if she was worthless because she'd lost her voice. The fury welled up again, traveling through his veins, curling his hands into fists.

Walk away. Now. Before you do something you'll regret.

He pivoted and grabbed Evangeline's hand to escape in the opposite direction. They'd only taken a couple of steps when the men skirted them, blocking their path again.

"Hey, what's your hurry?" the short one asked and leered at Evangeline, his gaze on her legs. "We're just doing our job."

If the smarmy little rat didn't get his dirty mind out of the gutter, Matthew would remove it from his skull. Through his nose. "Insulting people who are trying to walk down the street is not your job."

"No, satisfying the public's curiosity is. And we're all curious. What's Eva up to now? Who's the mysterious man escorting her around Venice?" The taller one shoved a small recorder at Matthew, nearly chipping a tooth. "You tell us. We leave. Easy."

"We already said—" Matthew backhanded the recorder away "—no comment."

He shrugged. "Then we'll write our own story. Eva does Venice with an American schoolteacher on holiday. Eva's

new beau—disinherited playboy after her money? Eva
sleeps her way into a modeling contra—"

Matthew's fist connected with the reporter's smug mouth.
He reeled backward, smashing into the other reporter.

God, that had felt good. He shook out his throbbing
knuckles.

The man regained his balance, touched his bleeding lip
and glanced at his fingers. "I'm pressing charges."

"See you in court. Until then, stay away from us."

He spun and herded Evangeline through the throng of
wide-eyed onlookers and down a side street free of people.
They didn't talk, but she grasped his tingling hand tightly.

His heart rate still in the upper stratosphere, he paused
in a dark alcove. "You okay?"

"Are *you*?" She touched his face, tentatively. "I've never
seen you like that."

"Never been like that." He'd never punched anyone in his
life. Not even Lucas, though his brother had surely asked
for it on many an occasion. Matthew handled conflict with
his brain. Usually. Nothing with Evangeline worked like
usual. "The things they were saying were hurtful. No one
has the right to treat you that way."

She melted into his arms. "Thank you," she murmured
against his shoulder. "I can't tell you what that meant to me."

It had been pure reaction. No thought to consequences.
No reason involved. Just a ferocious drive to protect Evangeline from being hurt.

He held her close and his pulse shuddered anew. Amber
would have been horrified. Not grateful. Amber didn't let
much affect her and would have blown off reporters with
some practiced sound bite. He'd never had a reason to protect her. A reason to be jealous. A reason to feel like he was
dancing across a high wire with no net and not only craved
the danger but kept asking for more.

Amber was gone.

And if he didn't disentangle himself from Evangeline soon, the man Amber had married would be gone, too. Then who would he be?

The next afternoon, Evangeline stretched out on the couch with Matt's iPad and downloaded a fluffy beach-read novel to entertain her while he took a shower. She needed a distraction from the slimy swirl those reporters had put in her stomach. The media had been a part of her life for a long time, and they'd never bothered her until after the surgery.

Now they just made her sick—physically, deep inside.

When Matt came downstairs, hair still a little damp and darkly golden, she forgot about the story on the page and watched him cross the room. Delicious. He still made her shiver despite the fact that she knew exactly what was underneath that waffle-print shirt and jeans. Maybe because she knew.

But it wasn't the body that got her going.

Matt had jarred something loose the moment he smashed that reporter in the face. It was far more than what he'd done with *Milano Sera*'s people. That had been simply an extraction. The incident with the reporters—something else entirely. She'd never felt anything like it, the rush of release, the empowerment of knowing he valued her enough to stand up to the evils of the world.

He had her back. No one ever had before.

"Busy?" he asked.

"Nope." She laid the tablet on the coffee table.

What could possibly compete with his attention? She loved being his focal point, morning, noon and night. Sure these were extraordinary circumstances, but no doubt he operated the same in real life, with his full commitment on whatever was in front of him. Matt did everything wholeheartedly.

"Do you know if Vincenzo is home today?"

She shrugged. "I think so. I saw him come home early

this morning when I was washing the breakfast dishes. I doubt he's even awake yet. Why?"

"I'm having something delivered. A surprise. Call him and ask if you can hang out over there for an hour. No peeking, either." With a mischievous smile, he snagged her hand and crossed her heart for her.

The area under her fingertip lurched sweetly. "A surprise? For me? What is it?"

He shook his head and mimed zipping his lips. "You'll see soon enough. Call."

Mystified and with no small amount of curiosity, she woke Vincenzo from his postdebauchery sleep and announced she was coming over.

Vincenzo answered the door with a bad case of bedhead and a worse attitude. She flounced past him into the living room and perched on the sofa. "You don't have to entertain me. Go back to bed."

Their friendship went back a couple of years, hinging on a mutual love of parties and a glittering social scene, but it had never been deep and meaningful. Like most of her relationships. Except one.

He eyed her. "Trouble in paradise, *cara*?"

"What, you mean between me and Matt?" She flicked off his concern with a wave. "He's surprising me with something."

She'd told Vincenzo very little about her relationship with Matt. On purpose. It didn't have the same transcendence when explained to an outsider.

Vincenzo jiggled his dark brows. "An engagement ring?"

Automatically, she started to deny it. But what if it was? No. Surely not. Venice was a temporary arrangement.

"He'd stick that in his pocket. Wouldn't he?"

She glanced at her hand, bare of jewelry since she'd ripped off Rory's ring and flushed it. Matt wasn't proposing. No way. He was looking for a way home, not a new wife. There were too many ghosts flitting through his heart for that.

"I am not an expert in matters of marriage." Vincenzo lifted one shoulder and shuffled in the direction of the marble staircase to the second floor, calling out, "Lock the door when you leave."

Alone, she contemplated what she'd say if Matt did get down on one knee and claimed he'd gotten over Amber....

He couldn't. If he did, she'd have to say no, and their affair would be over. Marriage—she couldn't imagine anything she'd be more ill-suited for.

She fretted about it until he texted her to come home.

When she burst in the door of Palazzo D'Inverno, the surprise nearly knocked her off her feet.

"Oh, my God."

A shiny, ebony grand piano stood in the corner of the living room, overlooking the Grand Canal. Matt sat on the bench, quietly watching her, and the two together put a glitch in her lungs she couldn't breathe through.

"Presumptuous of me, I realize," he said. "But I thought you might enjoy having it to play since going out isn't so fun."

Her fingers curled spontaneously. She hadn't touched piano keys since the surgery. Hadn't wanted to. Didn't want to now.

"Thanks. It's...nice."

His eyebrows rose. "You're welcome, and you seem a little underwhelmed. Did I screw up?"

Vehemently, she shook her head. "It's the most thoughtful gift anyone's ever given me."

"Okay. I'll take that." He slid off the bench and engulfed her in his warm, safe arms. "But there's more. Do you want to tell me, or is the piano now the armadillo in the room?"

The laugh slipped out. "How did you know I was going to call armadillo?"

"You get this closed-in face whenever you're about to say it."

"I don't want to play." It fell out of her mouth. Maybe on accident, or maybe because she couldn't bear for him to be so understanding and not get anything for it.

"You don't have to. I can send it back." He hugged her tighter and then released her. "I'll call the delivery company right now."

"No." That had definitely been said on purpose. She was safe with Matt. She knew that. "*Want* is the wrong word. I can't play."

"Like you've forgotten how?"

"Like the music is a razor blade." *Cut*, Madam Wong had said. The music had been cut from her throat and it cut when she heard it and it cut when she played.

"*Screw up* would be too kind a phrase, then," he said. "I'm sorry. I didn't know it was hard for you to play. I envisioned you gaining something…I don't know, peaceful from it."

Her eyelids shut in sudden memory. The piano had been her refuge in a lonely house growing up, the one thing her mother had given her. Because it was the path to fame and fortune, foremost, but Evangeline turned it into something else. A means of expression she'd channeled in conjunction with her voice. Always together.

The piano still had the music inside. She didn't. But in Palazzo D'Inverno, there were no rules, and the two didn't have to coexist. They could have value individually.

"I'd like to find some peace," she admitted. "I don't know why it's so hard."

"Peace is elusive."

She'd meant playing the piano was hard. He'd cut through the outer layer and exposed the raw truth. But not the whole truth. "Not when I'm with you."

With a smile, he captured her hand and pulled her toward the piano. "Then let's do it together."

"What? You don't play."

But he situated himself on the bench and drew her between his spread legs, placing her fingers on the keys under his own. "Teach me. I've been listening to music my whole life. How hard can it be?"

She snorted out a giggle and leaned back against the solid chest supporting her, his breath teasing her ear and his heart thumping her spine.

Safe. Matt was her anchor in a sea of anxiety.

"Move your hands. That's not how you learn. Here, listen."

Slowly, she picked out the notes to "Twinkle, Twinkle Little Star." The keys sank under her fingers with measured float, producing rich tones from under the raised lid. This was easily a hundred-thousand-dollar piano. And Matt had given it to her because he wanted her to experience peace by gently prodding her toward something she could still do.

She didn't mind that kind of push so much.

"A little elementary of a song choice, don't you think?" he said into her ear, and she elbowed him.

"Try it, smart guy. Go ahead." She nodded to the keys.

He plunked out a few scraggly notes that sounded more like he was dragging a screaming flamingo down the street than playing a song. But he got about half of them right—a hundred percent more than she was expecting.

"Not bad. Practice makes perfect."

"Show me another one." He nudged her with his chin, peering over her shoulder intently at the spread of white and black keys. "Something that takes both hands."

Without prompting, her fingers spread, arranging themselves around middle C and the melody trickled out. Then gained strength as her muscles remembered how to stretch and fly.

Matt's hand crept across her stomach and he held her tight as she played, never once flinching if her elbow caught him. He'd held her through a lot of difficult stuff. Had since the very first moments in the alcove at Vincenzo's party.

When the last notes faded, she slumped, drained.

"One of yours?" he asked softly.

"The first one I ever recorded." But on a synthesizer and with a faster tempo, when she'd had the energy of a burgeoning career to fuel her performance. "My fingers are tired."

His lips rested against her temple. "You don't have to play anymore. Though I enjoyed every second of it."

"It's a good kind of tired. Thanks for playing with me. It helped." The armadillos were having a throw-down in her stomach, but after last night, the exposure of being Eva again and sitting here at the piano, it was too much to keep from bubbling over. "It more than helped. I'm reminded again of what music means to me."

Reminded again of the peace of simple expression, which had been impossible, until lately.

"What does it mean?"

Escape, she thought. Music had been an escape. It could be again, in a far different way. She could separate music from Eva, peel back that layer and see what was underneath. Eva was gone. Evangeline could be herself.

"It means I have choices."

"You did a brave thing by playing the piano again." It was a gentle echo of what she'd said to him during the middle-of-the-night, nothing-is-sacred conversation. "It was hard, but you did it. Choose to do something else difficult. Write a song for Sara Lear."

"I'll think about it."

"Good." It was all he'd say. Somehow, that encouraged her to fill the silence.

"The music industry…" She cleared her raspy throat— a wasted effort. "It'll rob you of everything you'd hoped to gain. The fame, the money…I readily admit I loved that part. But there's a price. You lose a sense of yourself and who you are without all the costume changes. People don't see you anymore. Not the fans. Not the execs. Both put you on a pedestal but watch to see if you teeter just a tiny bit. Then the new song doesn't climb the charts as fast as the last one. The fans are fickle, and the producers mutter about profits."

It was a no-win catch-22. Everyone wanted a piece of her until they were done with her. Rory. The industry. And everyone eventually rejected her, even people who should love her no matter what.

"I see you," he murmured.

She nodded. "That's why I'm still here."

Matt made it safe to ditch the mask and be herself. He was the one man on earth she could trust with the deepest part of herself and not be braced for a rejection because she wasn't good enough.

He was the only one who could get her to stay because for the first time in her life, staying was better than leaving.

Ten

Moonlight poured through the panes of glass in the bedroom. Evangeline eased out from under Matt's arm and pulled the covers over his gorgeously muscled torso. He shifted but didn't wake up.

She watched him breathe, unable to tear her eyes away. Sooty lashes brushed his cheeks, and underneath those lids lay the most amazing depths. No matter how many mornings she woke wound up in his long limbs, it wouldn't be enough. She could stand here forever and bask in his presence.

But the words were flowing, calling her with their siren song, begging her to commit the emotion to paper. She couldn't ignore the first stirring of inspiration.

The piano had unwound something inside her, and Matt patiently drew it out, helping her examine it in his clear-headed, logical way.

Downstairs, she plopped onto the couch with the back of a take-out menu and a pen. Fifteen minutes later, lyrics covered every blank space on the menu. Good lyrics. For the first time in *months*, she'd tapped into her center and captured the music.

She rummaged around for more paper and came up empty-handed. Matt's iPad sat on the coffee table and though under normal circumstances she'd never use a digital page, she couldn't lose momentum.

When she hit the power button, one of the squares with the logo WFP caught her attention. It hadn't been there before.

She touched it and the website popped up. Wheeler Family Partners. The header contained the profiles of four men and she recognized Matt's instantly. The chiseled good-looking face next to Matt must be his brother, Lucas. A total player. She could see the look in his eye a mile away and hoped his wife kept that one on a short leash.

The other men must be their dad and grandfather. Andrew and Robert, according to the About page. Matt favored his grandfather. They both had the same piercing gaze and straightforwardness. She could tell neither of them would ever lie, cheat or steal.

Her eye wandered down the paragraph. Geez. Wheeler Family Partners had done eighty million dollars of business in the last quarter of the previous year alone, largely owing to the sale of a communications complex in North Dallas.

And Matt had been the spearhead of his firm. Like she'd assumed, he'd been successful at everything he'd tried. Business. Marriage. Getting her to stay.

He was far more special than she'd imagined.

She tapped the website closed and brought up a free-text application, more than a little concerned she'd stemmed the fountain of words with her side foray into Matt's domain.

A blank page materialized. It didn't scare her.

But the words she typed did. She couldn't stop, didn't even pause as the song fell from her fingers, fully formed. Whereas the first round had taken shape in bits and pieces, this one had structure. Order. And it would be a guaranteed hit. She knew it. All four of her Grammys had been for songwriting, not singing.

The piano hovered in the corner of her peripheral vision, and she glanced up at it, then up the stairs to where Matt lay sleeping. No piano this time. She didn't want to wake him.

The fortune teller had predicted she'd conceive. And this felt like birth, like the beginning of something wonderful and amazing. A metamorphosis.

As the last word appeared, she finally removed her fingers from the screen and read over the song again, hearing the tune in her head as she internalized the words. With the right voice, like Sara Lear's, it would climb the charts instantly.

She saved the file to her cloud account and powered off the tablet, staring out the window at the quiet canal.

The right voice. It wouldn't be hers. She wasn't ready to let the song go to another home, but for the first time, it didn't sting so badly to envision it. Thanks to Matt.

Here in the dark, it didn't seem so frightening to admit she was falling for him. He was so genuine and real, and her stupid heart hungrily latched onto those qualities. She knew better. Knew that nothing could crumble the monument to Amber in his chest. But her heart had its fingers in its ears, refusing to hear the message from her brain.

Matt was a heartbreak waiting to happen.

She should go before it was too late. Nicola had a place in Monte Carlo. Vincenzo had been making noises about shoving off in that direction in a few days and had texted her the address with an open invitation to join the group. Her stomach rolled. It had been off since the reporter incident.

Matt still needed her. His turmoil churned below the surface, popping up in his faraway gaze at odd moments. She'd give anything to ease that note of sheer anguish in his voice when he talked about his family and the life he'd lost.

She didn't want to leave.

Her head fell back against the couch cushion. The riot of colors splashed across the ceiling was dim with only the outside canal lights to illuminate it. The paintings depicted domestic vignettes; men and women sleeping, eating, playing with children. This had been someone's refuge, built to escape a harsh climate.

She and Matt had both done the same. And despite what she told herself about the reasons she stayed, she needed him as much as he needed her. How much longer could they hide away here before Venice became a stumbling block to healing instead of a sanctuary?

Matt's gentle hands in her hair woke her. Daylight streamed through the panes leading to the balcony and beyond the glass, Venice was awash with the morning.

"You okay?" Matt asked from behind her. "Why didn't you come back to bed?"

"Meant to. But I fell asleep." She yawned. The mist of sleep would not clear her mind, like she'd dunked her head in a vat of Jell-O.

"I'll make you some breakfast."

Food did not sound appealing in the least. "You go ahead. I'm going to take a shower. I'll grab something later."

He leaned to plant an upside-down kiss on her lips. "Want me to scrub your back?"

Which was code for Very-Little-Bathing-To-Occur. "Normally I'd be all over that. But I'm just wiped out. The shower is to wake me up." She smiled to soften the blow.

"If you're sure." He brushed a thumb tenderly across her temple and disappeared into the kitchen. Thumps of cabinets opening and dishes clinking drifted out. Comforting sounds. Sounds of home.

How would she know? She'd never had the kind of home the noises had evoked. Never wanted one.

Until now.

Oh, God, where had that come from? This wasn't her home. It wasn't even Matt's home. Home was for people who wanted to stay together, who implicitly trusted each other and never spent all their energy looking for the exit.

She didn't do the domestic thing for a reason. And her subconscious argued that the reason was because she hadn't done it with the right person yet.

Heavy with fatigue, she wandered upstairs to take a long hot shower and get dressed. Somewhere along the way, she began to feel human again. By the time she returned to the lower level, Matt was watching cable news with the crinkle in his forehead that meant he was bored.

When he caught sight of her, he lit up, his expression radiant, and he was absolutely the most gorgeous man on earth. Her heart squished. Out of nowhere, lines of a new song popped into her head. A sappy, sugary love song.

She wasn't just falling for him, she'd splatted flat on the ground and then a giant cupid had stepped on her.

"Feeling better?" he asked.

"Define *better*," she mumbled, eyes closed in case her stupid, inadvisable feelings were beaming from her insides. "I'm awake, if that's what you mean."

He leaped off the couch and hustled her into the kitchen so he could ply her with food, though the thought of putting anything in her mouth made her slightly nauseous.

Idiot reporters. Those creeps were still upsetting her. She didn't say anything. There was no point in Matt being upset, too.

Gulping orange juice, she took a seat at the island and watched Matt move around the kitchen. Poetry in motion. He was never content to shove a couple of pieces of bread in the toaster and call it breakfast. His idea of cooking involved creativity usually reserved for master chefs.

Today, he was making an egg-white omelet with prosciutto and sun-dried tomatoes, and a half-moon of cantaloupe on the side. He placed the plate in front of her with a flourish and refilled her empty orange juice glass.

She forked a bite into her mouth and swallowed. It stayed down. "Delicious. As always. You should open a restaurant."

"Nah. I just throw some stuff together and pray it turns out." He waved it off with a pleased smile. "Cooking is fun."

"I'm glad one of us thinks so." Her idea of fun was paying someone else to cook. And clean up the kitchen. Matt had never met a pan unworthy of his olive oil or chicken stock. But he made such fantastic dishes, she really didn't mind cleaning up.

"Well, I never used to." He shrugged. "But I like cooking for you."

"Why, because I'm so inventive with how I show my appreciation?" She waggled her brows.

He laughed. "That is one of the perks. But mostly because you let me. Amber...she was kind of a Gordon Ramsay about her kitchen. I stayed out of it."

The omelet took on a whole new significance. "You never cooked for Amber?"

"Sure, when we were dating. But then, I don't know. She loved to cook and prided herself on it, so I just didn't anymore." He stared out the window at the joint courtyard Palazzo D'Inverno shared with Vincenzo's house, his gaze faraway and dejected. "I paid through the nose to upgrade the kitchen in this place. For her. I didn't expect to be the one who would actually use it. Honestly, I probably never would have started cooking again if you hadn't stayed."

That put a lump the size of a grapefruit in her throat. She couldn't swallow. "Thanks for resurrecting your spatula for me."

He shot her a grin. Lately, it didn't take long at all for him to snap out of his Amber mood, which, if she had her way, he'd get out of permanently.

"You eat too much takeout. Or you used to. You were practically wasted away to nothing when I got ahold of you. At least this way, I know you're putting something healthy into your body."

"Oh, I see. You cook for me because you're concerned about my health," she joked back.

And then it sank in. It wasn't a joke. He'd been taking care of her. All along. Maybe subconsciously she'd known that and hence had begun to equate kitchen sounds with a sense of home.

Matt communicated in subtle, baffling ways she'd never experienced—probably because she never stayed long enough to allow it. What was he trying to tell her with food? That he might have deeper and more lasting feelings for her then she'd thought?

Wishful thinking at its worst.

Her eyes burned with the sudden prick of tears.

The omelet turned to mush in her mouth, and she shoved the plate away. "I didn't get much sleep last night. Think I'll go back to bed."

"Are you coming down with something?" He skirted the island and cupped her chin with both palms to peer into her eyes, concern practically dripping from his touch.

"I'm fine. Just tired."

Narrowed blue eyes locked onto hers. The deflection didn't fool him, but he chose not to call her on it.

Upstairs, she threw herself onto the bed, but it smelled like Matt and that wasn't conducive to sleep, unless she wanted to have red-hot dreams about the way that man's mouth felt on her body. She'd rather be experiencing the real thing, but with something far stronger than desire in his gaze.

She wanted Amber's place in his heart. It was a really inadvisable thing to long for. But that didn't make the longing magically disappear.

Matt had cooked for her. He'd been taking care of her in a way he never had with Amber.

Maybe he just needed more time to get over her. Maybe being here, in the house he'd bought his wife, prevented Matt from fully healing. Was Evangeline falling down on her job by dragging out their Venice bubble?

She rolled over and buried her face in the pillow, exhausted but unable to shut off the hamsters turning the wheel in her brain. She'd never been so tired in her life, probably because she'd rendered herself completely inactive. This was the longest she'd stayed in one place.

Monte Carlo beckoned. The words—the music—flowed again after a long, painful hiatus. If she stayed, all that lovely inspiration might dry up again. The wind had always guided her well enough before.

But if she moved on, Matt might lose all the progress he'd made. Worse, they'd never find out what might be possible between them. He couldn't go home yet; that much he'd made clear in more than one conversation.

What if they moved on together?

A daring question. But what if it worked?

If she said the idea of being loved by Matt didn't thrill her, she'd be lying. A solid, committed man like Matt would never fail her, and in turn, she'd never fail him. They had an unparalleled measure of trust in each other, an understanding. That was the way love was supposed to work. She wanted that, for once in her life.

But what if she asked and he said no? He'd been drifting in search of a way to get his old life back. Just because he wasn't ready to go home this minute didn't mean that goal had changed. Could she really risk Matt's rejection?

After mulling it over for a long time, sleep finally claimed her.

Matthew's slight restless feeling graduated into a full-blown itch to do something productive. He settled for getting out of the house.

He took his laptop to the rooftop patio and sat in the sun. The Venetian spring was unbelievable, still cool in the mornings, but a warm breeze wafted from the Adriatic Sea, laden with the pungent scent of marine life.

He wished Evangeline had come up to enjoy it with him,

but she was taking an afternoon nap for the third time in a week.

Something was up, and he suspected she slept to avoid him. Because she was leaving. He could feel her winding down, becoming less talkative.

Honestly, he was avoiding "the talk," too. It didn't feel finished, this thing between them, but only because he didn't want it to be. For once, the idea of no commitment seemed like a blessing. There would be no broken heart in his future when she took off.

The organ in question gave a quick, painful tug at the thought of Evangeline leaving, and he shut his eyes until it started beating normally again. *No more of that, now.*

Since he had an afternoon to himself, Matthew poked around in his stock accounts, balanced his checkbook and generally killed time with stuff that had no promise of holding his interest.

He logged onto WFP, curious to see if anything new was going on. Lucas had posted a few sales, but nothing major and certainly not at the same clip as his brother had performed last quarter. First quarter historically saw the best sales as companies began the year with clean budgets.

The numbers should be better.

Strategies, marketing, building specs—all of it scrolled into his head and he latched on greedily, gratified both the knowledge and the drive was still there.

They could easily gain visibility by—

Stay out of it.

Lucas was handling it, as he had been. What good could Matthew possibly do from halfway around the world?

Renewed guilt gnawed on his insides.

Real estate was in his blood, and he'd missed the negotiations, the deals, the art of reading a potential seller. But the restlessness was more than lack of a job; it was a lack of setting goals and working to achieve them. Feeling successful and knowing his effort would be rewarded tangibly.

He wanted to be dependable, responsible Matthew Wheeler again, not a grieving, guilt-ridden widower.

Maybe he could check in, casually, without throwing his weight around. That might work. He was still a partner, regardless of whether he'd been acting like one, and there was no time like the present to start making amends.

Evangeline had played the piano. Maybe he could take a step out of the valley, too.

A baby step. The top of the mountain would grow closer with each one.

Before he thought better of it, he fished out his phone and sent Lucas a text message.

The response came instantly. You're alive?

Matthew flinched. Yeah, he deserved that. He shot back: Still have a pulse last time I checked. What's going on with WFP? 1st Q looks like a train wreck.

What do you care?

I care. I'll send flowers to soothe your bruised feelings later. 1st Q?

Lucas's answer took almost five minutes, during which Matthew sweated through some very unpleasant possibilities, like Lucas had fallen off the responsibility wagon or something had happened to their father.

Richards Group opened shop in Dallas.

Matthew swore. That had never crossed his mind.

Saul Richards owned the Houston real-estate market and the Wheelers owned North Texas. It was understood that Richards stayed on his turf and the Wheelers stayed on theirs. The shift wasn't a mystery—Richards had scented Wheeler blood with Matthew out of the picture.

Matthew shouldn't be out of the picture. Lucas had been

handling it. Now he needed help. Wheeler Family Partners had been in business for over a century, and Matthew refused to be the one who let it fail.

It was time to go home.

The thought didn't fill him with dread like he'd expected. His life in Dallas had been inescapably intertwined with Amber, with the expectations of creating a family and upholding traditions. But she was gone and as he'd flippantly, but accurately, told Lucas, he still had a pulse. Lucas had married a wife who helped him succeed, and they were happily working on the continuation of the Wheeler line.

There was no pressure for Matthew to fill his old role until he was ready.

The healing had happened so gradually, he hadn't realized it.

Evangeline called his name, and he glanced up to see her waltzing across the patio from the stairs. Sunlight beamed across her face, and she smiled. It slid down his throat with a jagged edge and sliced something in his gut.

God Almighty, she was almost ethereal. But sexy. Strong. Luminous.

Fingers numb, he dropped his phone to the concrete and pulled her into his lap to kiss her thoroughly. She smelled like sleep and Evangeline and everything good in the world. She'd helped him heal. Brightened up his house. His soul.

As the familiar lightning-fast rush of heat filled him, it suddenly occurred to him that if he went home, he'd have to end things with Evangeline.

Then he had the most dangerous thought—what if she came home with him?

No. He couldn't fathom issuing such an invitation. An invitation for what? To hide away in some lover's nest while he stormed the gates of Saul Richards's blockade on the Dallas real-estate market? She would grow bored with Dallas in about five minutes. She'd grow bored with Matthew Wheeler in four.

He could imagine going home for the first time in a long time. But he could not imagine Evangeline there, fitting into Amber's role as the woman behind the Wheeler. Mostly because bright, glittery Evangeline could never blend into the background the way Amber had, quietly providing support and encouragement, organizing get-togethers and charity events with his mother. The women in his world were beige.

Evangeline shifted in his lap, straddling him, her tongue finding creative ways to tease him. Yeah, she was as far from beige as Venice was from Dallas, and he forgot about everything but the warm breeze on his face and the hot woman in his arms.

She drew back, breathing heavily, with a businesslike glint in her eye. "I came to talk. Stop distracting me."

Talk. That sounded bad.

He scooted her back an inch, off his blazing erection, in deference to the directive. "Hey, I'm not the one looking all sexy and disheveled and climbing all over you."

"Can't help myself," she murmured and sighed, thrusting her chest into his. "You're so tempting."

She wasn't wearing a bra and talking was pretty much the last thing he wanted to do.

"What did you want to talk about?" he asked, and snaked a hand under her T-shirt, which was actually his, and hell if that wasn't the most arousing thing ever. He fanned a palm across her bare back, gradually working it around to the front where her breast fell into his eager fingers.

She moaned and arched against him. "Monte Carlo."

He paused, thumb and forefinger wrapped firmly around her nipple. "What about it?"

The end of things now had definition. She was going to Monte Carlo, and he did not want to think about all the implications.

"There's a party." She gasped. "Don't stop. Whatever you're doing, it feels amazing."

"You mean this?" Tweaking her nipple again, he shoved

her up against his erection because maybe they were going to talk *and* have sex. It would be the first time in several days they'd connected outside of bed.

"Yes. That." She writhed against him, igniting his flesh. His eyes crossed. "I didn't bring a condom. Fair warning."

"Well, now. That sounds like a challenge. Hmm. What can I do that doesn't require a condom?" He yanked the T-shirt up and closed a nipple between his lips, sucking for all he was worth. Her warm skin felt like velvet in his mouth and she moaned his name, bucking against him.

He loved her responses, loved that *he* could do that to her.

He slipped a thumb down her shorts and inside her panties to circle her trigger-point, and relentlessly pleasured her until she came apart. Beautiful. He could watch that over and over.

Boneless, she slumped against him, and he breathed through his nose until his erection subsided to merely painful instead of excruciating.

"You were telling me about a party?" he prompted when her breathing slowed.

This was it. She was taking off. Maybe later today. This might be their last time together.

He did not want to give her up.

"I was?" She rolled her head to nuzzle his neck, nearly sending him off the edge of the chair.

"In Monte Carlo. Talk fast because we're finishing this in about four seconds downstairs." He stood with her in his arms, sad it was over.

No, not sad. Devastated.

"Um…" She met his gaze and smiled, but it never reached her eyes. "Never mind. We can talk about it later. Take me downstairs."

Swallowing, he nodded. She didn't want to ruin their last time together with unpleasant reminders of what was about to happen. Neither did he.

Evangeline was the best thing that had ever happened to

him, enlivening him, encouraging him—but also encouraging him to keep hiding. To keep being a runaway.

It was best to go their separate ways, like they'd always planned. Lucas needed him, and the sting of reentering his old life without Amber had mellowed. When he went home, Matt would disappear forever, and there'd be no more wild and crazy, totally-un-Matthew-like Venetian affairs. He'd have his identity back. A plan. Security.

Evangeline would be free to fly off wherever she chose to go next, chasing the wind to the ends of the Earth.

The thought should have made him happier.

Venice was a transitory interlude, and now it was done. He only wished that truth eased the tightness in his lungs. And in his heart.

If only….well, life didn't give anyone the luxury of "if only."

When he picked up his phone to follow Evangeline back to the lower level, he saw another text from Lucas.

I'm handling Richards. Don't worry your pretty little head about it.

Eleven

Evangeline stared at the half-packed suitcase blindly and gnawed on a fingernail. Not one of her previously mani-cured-within-an-inch-of-their-lives fingernails remained.

Matt had gone for a walk. By himself. She didn't blame him for dealing with reality in his own way. Venice, the temporary fix, was over. It just didn't feel like it should be, and if things went the way she hoped, it wouldn't have to be.

She'd almost asked him to go to Monte Carlo. It had been right there on the tip of her tongue, but at the last mo-ment, she couldn't chance a "no," not after he so cleverly steered her away from talking about it. He didn't *want* to talk about it.

But she had a hunch they'd be doing nothing but talking by the time he came back from his walk, because something huge and frightening and momentous might have happened and it sat right in the middle of her consciousness, scream-ing its presence. All she had to do was verify it.

The doorbell chimed.

Evangeline bolted downstairs and grabbed the package from the delivery guy, slammed the door in his face and only remembered she'd forgotten to tip him after she locked herself in the bathroom.

Hands shaking, she pulled the pregnancy test from the brown wrapper. It was pretty much a formality. Icing on a cake that had already been baking for over a month, since the no-condom roof incident. The fatigue, the slight nausea, the way she sometimes couldn't get enough of Matt's hands on her overly sensitized body and other times, couldn't stand for him to touch her at all—it meant something much more weighty than a need to move on.

This morning, she'd done the math, then called the pharmacy the second Matt went for his walk. Bless him for his foresight in setting up a delivery account, though she doubted either of them could have envisioned it would prevent unwanted photographs of Eva buying a pregnancy test.

Two minutes passed in a blur, and her life changed forever when the little plus sign appeared as expected.

A sob bubbled from her throat, but it was half shaky excitement and half disbelief. Madam Wong's prediction that she'd conceive had encompassed more than songs.

A baby. She was going to have a baby. Matt's baby.

It would be a girl, with Matt's beautiful blue eyes and her voice. Her heart fluttered. Of course. This baby could be the answer to her future. She couldn't sing, but she could learn to be a mom.

And Matt would be a dad, father to their baby. She'd be giving him the one thing Amber never could—the family he wanted. He'd forget about his wife in a heartbeat, like she never existed, and come with Evangeline to Monte Carlo.

Before, she and Matt didn't make sense long term. Now they did. The baby would clinch it. He'd never reject his own flesh and blood. She and Matt would be happy, deliriously in love, with the proof of Matt's devotion strapped into a baby-carrier on his back.

They'd *both* have a family. Together.

Okay, she was getting ahead of herself. She had to tell

him first. But there was no doubt this would be the catalyst to keep them together. No doubt he'd be thrilled. He'd drifted into her life for a reason—to heal, surely, but also to move on with the next phase of life.

Evangeline was his next phase.

When his key rattled in the lock, she jumped up from the couch to greet the father of her child. A powerful twist of emotion welled up, like she'd never felt before. She tried to emblazon it in her memory so she could get it into a song as soon as possible.

"Hey," he said. "I'm glad you're still here. I got you something."

"Funny. I have something for you, too." Did she sound giddy?

His grin arrowed straight to her heart. "You do? What is it?"

She shook her head. "You first."

Pulling a wrapped box from a bag, he dropped it into her cupped hands. "To remember me by."

Wait until she told him he'd already given her the greatest memento possible.

The wrapping paper hit the floor. Jewelry. She flipped the hinged velvet lid and gasped.

"Wow. That was not what I was expecting. I love it."

It was a white enameled Carnevale mask, painted with delicate brush strokes in a rainbow of colors. Teardrop diamonds spilled from the eyes. She pinned it to her shirt, over her heart.

He grazed the mask with a fingertip and glanced up. "I'm glad. I wanted you to have something unusual but easily carried. Since you move around a lot."

That nearly knocked her to the floor. "Thanks. It means a lot that you understand me."

"I'm trying to." He cocked his head. "What did you get me?"

"My gift is unusual but easily carried, too. I hope you'll like it as much."

She hadn't wrapped hers. Fishing it from her pocket, she handed over the pregnancy test.

"What is it?" He took it with a puzzled expression.

Then his whole body stiffened. His expression, his eyes, everything went absolutely still.

"You're pregnant?" he asked hoarsely, gaze flitting back and forth between her and the plus sign. "The naps. Drinking orange juice like it's going out of style. You're pregnant."

"And you're going to be a father." She couldn't keep the smile off her face. "Congratulations."

Matt sank onto the couch as if he hadn't heard her, still staring at the piece of plastic in his hands. "So I assume this means you're keeping it."

Horrified, she glared at him. "As if there was a possibility I might not? Of course I'm keeping it."

"Okay." He blew out a breath and rubbed his forehead absently, not looking at her. "Okay. I just wanted to make sure I understood. That's the right decision. But I'll support you no matter what."

"I never had a doubt."

Matt wasn't like her father. He was solid, capable. Not weak. Matt was a forever kind of guy and somehow, she'd been lucky enough to find him. A baby changed everything. It gave him more than enough reason to move on. With her.

"It was that time on the roof. Wasn't it? When we forgot the condoms." He looked a little green around the edges. "You said it was the wrong time of the month."

"I thought it was. I miscalculated. But it was already too late, and honestly, I'm glad. We're having a baby and I'm looking forward to being a mom. How do you feel about being a dad?"

Matt shut his eyes. "You've had a little more time to process than me. Give me a minute. Can I get you a drink? Crackers?" He shoved both hands behind his neck, like he was trying to hold his head in place. "I don't even know what to do for a pregnant woman. Be right back."

She watched him flee, breath rattling in her throat, cutting off all her oxygen as she reevaluated his reaction. It never occurred to her that he wouldn't welcome the news. He'd always wanted a family, hadn't he?

Well, he'd said he needed a minute. She had no choice but to give it to him. When he came back, he'd be ready to talk about the future, and then they could make plans to go to Monte Carlo.

Everything was going to be great.

Matthew escaped to the kitchen, formerly his haven. The place where he went to create, feel productive.

Hands spread wide, he leaned on the counter, head down. There still didn't seem to be any blood circulating in his brain. The walls were too close together and the gap between them narrowed.

Pregnant.

Evangeline was *pregnant*.

He wasn't ready to think about being with Evangeline forever, wasn't prepared to examine why they still gelled when they shouldn't. Couldn't get past the fear that suddenly not one, but two people could easily become the center of his existence. Only to be ripped away.

This was his reward for flagrantly disregarding the rules and living in the moment with no thought to consequences. This was what running away from life had gotten him.

Automatically, he filled a glass full of water and downed it without coming up for air once.

From here on out, he'd have to do the right thing. Ironically, if he'd been doing the right thing all along, this never would have happened. But he was a Wheeler, first and foremost, and it was far past time to start acting like one.

What was he going to do? Evangeline would never fit

into his life in Dallas. But she had to. Because he had to. Neither of them had a choice any longer.

Something rushed through his heart. *Relief.* They didn't have a choice but to make it work, whether he was ready to think about forever or not. Forever had started the moment she spoke to him in Vincenzo's hall. Venice was over, but they could still be together.

He returned to the living room, calm and in control. He hoped.

He sat on the couch next to Evangeline. "I'm sorry. I'm one hundred percent here now."

But minus a drink for her. Maybe he was more like ninety percent here.

"I'm glad." Her eyes were enormous and shiny. Red. She'd been crying and it wrenched his heart. No matter what he was going through, it hardly compared to an emotional *and* physical wallop, like what had happened to her.

Stop thinking about yourself, Wheeler.

"Hey," he said softly and took her hand. "It's going to be okay. Did I make you cry? I didn't mean to."

She shook her head. "I'm all emotional. From hormones, I guess. I've never been pregnant before."

"It'll be fine. I'll be here for you. Take you to the doctor and—" he swallowed against the sudden burn in his throat "—be in the delivery room to cut the umbilical cord."

All things he'd looked forward to doing with Amber. Seeing his wife rounded with their child. Lacing fingers as they watched the image in the sonogram. Never had he imagined it happening with someone else, and *never* would he have anticipated the spike of unadulterated elation at the thought of doing it with Evangeline.

Ruthlessly, he shut off the emotions careening through his chest. Becoming emotional would not help this situation.

"So we're going to be together?" she asked tentatively, and her grip on his hand tightened. "You want to be a part of the baby's life?"

The baby's life. He shook his head, to clear it, to whack something loose that made sense. How would anything make sense ever again?

There was so much more to consider than the pregnancy. The next eight months were only the beginning. He and Evangeline were going to be parents, of a kid who would eventually walk and talk and learn to ride a bike.

A baby. He was going to be a dad. Panic nearly blinded him—but the clearest sense of awe fought its way to the forefront.

"We'll raise it together. Of course we will."

The baby would be a Wheeler, entitled to everything Matthew could and would provide. The circumstances weren't ideal, and this curveball certainly jerked him back to reality.

Venice was *definitely* over. They needed to make plans, decisions. Find a place to live. Insurance. A car with a baby seat. His head spun. He didn't own a car anymore.

Evangeline gave him a watery smile. She was so thrilled, and he hated to squelch her enthusiasm, but they both needed to get real, really fast. Their relationship was now permanent. Two people who had almost nothing in common other than enormously painful events in their pasts were going to be parents.

"Together," she repeated. "I like the sound of that. There was something about you, from the very first, that called to me. The fortune-teller even predicted it. That we'd conceive. Remember?"

What he remembered was chasing down a beautiful butterfly for the sole purpose of feeling something again, and tripping headlong into an affair he'd believed would help him get back home. All he'd wished for was a sign that he'd make it back to his old self. That he might heal.

Instead, one passionate round of rooftop sex had bound him to this woman permanently. A woman who was so different from every woman he'd ever met and with whom *he* had to be different to even keep up.

As stakes in the ground went, she'd presented him with a doozy. A baby. The panic rose again, thick in his throat. He pushed it down.

They'd be together. They'd have a family. It was a blessing, no matter what.

"We can get married quietly." If they didn't have any guests, the date of their wedding didn't have to be publicized. They might be able to hide the fact that the baby was conceived out of wedlock. Anything to avoid causing his parents public embarrassment.

His back teeth clacked together. But he wouldn't lie to his parents—they'd have to know the truth. The vision he had in his head of sitting with Amber on his parent's sofa and gleefully telling them about the coming grandchild shattered. Of course, it had shattered long ago.

"Married? What are you talking about?"

"You're pregnant. We're getting married." Out of order. Once again.

She laughed. "Matt, we don't have to be married to be together. Love isn't dependent on a piece of paper."

Love? Did she think he was in love with her? Was she in love with *him*?

Evangeline made him crazy. She provoked sensual— okay, downright erotic—impulses from him. Pulled his soul from the deep freeze and made it okay to say whatever he wanted. Feel whatever he wanted. He couldn't do that forever. His life—his real life—had order and structure. No surprises. He had to get that back.

And he didn't want to be in love.

Never again. If he was doomed to suffer forever for falling in love with Amber, he certainly didn't want to repeat that mistake. Especially not with Evangeline, who made him feel so much. Especially not now.

How much harder would it be to love his child's mother and lose her?

The thought of losing either the mother or the child squeezed his chest so hard, he couldn't breathe. He cursed—was it already too late?

"A baby isn't dependent on love, either," he said. Harsh. But true. Neither of them could afford to keep up the fantasy they'd been living, and he needed to internalize that fact as much as she did. Real life wasn't about mystical connections and Venetian love affairs between incompatible people.

"We're getting married," he repeated.

Her eyebrows came together. "Who said I wanted to get married? You didn't even ask me."

He dismissed her words with a wave. "That's just a formality. Marriage will be good for you."

Her career was over—but she could be a wife and a mother. He had to make her see that. There was so much more to consider than whether he'd *asked* or not.

She recoiled as if he'd slapped her. "A formality? I deserve to be asked. With a ring. And you know, something along the lines of 'I love you and want to be with you the rest of my life.' Try it and then I'll give you my answer."

She was right. He'd gone about proposing the wrong way, but God Almighty, who could blame him? This humdinger of a development had flipped him inside out.

"I don't have a ring. As far as I knew, we were kissing each other goodbye today. I'm sorry." He took a deep breath and slid her palm to his mouth, kissing it in silent apology before he released it. "Let's figure out the next steps together."

She smiled. "The first step is to remember we're going to be happy."

Happy. Happiness had been a sheer impossibility when he left Dallas. But Evangeline had changed that.

They could be happy outside of Venice. Evangeline was amazing, strong, resilient. Look at how she'd walked into the lion's den of that horrific interview. Faced down the reporters. Played the piano. She could adapt to the role of Mrs. Wheeler and enjoy a life with roots. After all, they'd have a baby and a household to keep her busy and content.

She'd been searching for the next steps, and he'd give them to her. Being his wife would keep her demons away permanently, and she'd definitely become less…glittery. Then they'd gel in Dallas as well as they did here in Venice.

He returned her smile, and somehow it relaxed him. "Well, at least we already know we can live together without killing each other."

He didn't have to give her up. It was easier to picture her in Dallas if he forgot about all the reasons he and Evangeline wouldn't work and instead focused on what would be great.

"I'll let you cook. All the time. I have no problem with a man in my kitchen. It turns me on."

Her thumb smoothed over his and for the first time since he'd walked into the hornets' nest, he actually felt in control again.

Evangeline tucked her feet up under her and leaned into Matt's warm chest. Finally, things had clicked into place, and he'd lost that panicked edge, poor guy. She got that it was a little rough to have something so life-changing dropped on you out of the blue. The adjustment was still messing with her, too.

Marriage—of course he'd want that, and she was still contemplating it. If he came up with a really good proposal, she might actually say yes.

There was a shock. She'd thought Rory had crushed the desire for marriage out of her forever. But Matt wasn't like other men, and to him she was so much more than a broken voice.

"There's a lot to discuss," he said, and she nodded against his shoulder.

"First off, I'd like to talk about Monte Carlo." Thankfully, she hadn't brought it up yet. This way, it was practically a foregone conclusion. "The party is already in full swing but if we leave by Thurs—"

"What?" Matt tilted her head up to pierce her with a puzzled gaze. "We can't go to Monte Carlo. Especially not to a party."

"That's where all my friends are. We can tell everyone the news, and of course I can't drink any champagne, but you can have a glass for me."

It would be a fantastic way to celebrate. Not exactly the kind of party Vincenzo and his crowd were used to, but fun all the same. Maybe someone would volunteer to throw her a baby shower.

"We don't have to stay long," she added. "A week, tops. Then I suppose we can come back to Venice until the tourist season star—"

"There's no more Venice." His lips curved up in a half smile, maybe in apology for cutting her off *again*, but the rest of his face was pure confusion. "Surely you've realized that. We'll be flying to the States. We can leave as soon as you're ready. Somewhere along the way, I'll buy a ring and we'll get married at my parents' house."

A little discombobulated, she frowned. "I thought we already talked about the marriage proposal. And there still hasn't been one. Plus, I don't want to go to America. I hate it there. You think the press is bad in Italy, wait until you've dealt with the gossip websites."

"I don't want to deal with the press at all. Unfortunately we don't have that choice because America is where Dallas is and that's where we're going."

"Dallas? You want to go back to Dallas?" The harsh consonants rang in her ears. She'd always known that was his goal, but things had changed. *He* had changed. And he'd said more than once he didn't think he could go back yet. Monte Carlo was an opportunity to continue healing. "What's in Dallas for you?"

"Dallas is where my family is, my job," he explained, and his tone implied she should have already figured this out. "And that's where I have to live in order to do it. Also, my mother is there. She'll help you with the baby."

"I have a mother."

In a manner of speaking—she'd rather eat Brussels sprouts than ask her mom for parenting advice, and honestly, she might not mention the baby to her mother at all. Evangeline hadn't darkened the door of her mother's in a year or two. It wouldn't be out of the realm of possibility to keep the pregnancy from her.

"Your mother is welcome to come and stay for as long as you want her to," Matt offered, and she tried not to gag at the thought. "But my mother will be involved. I want her to have a relationship with her grandchild."

"There's an app for that. It's called Skype."

"That's ridiculous." He flicked off her suggestion as if she hadn't spoken. "I'll probably buy a house close to my parents. There's a good private school in their neighborhood. How early is too early to get on the waiting list, do you think?"

"Matt." He was babbling about something called Hockaday. It was like they were speaking two totally different languages. She tugged on his shirt. "Matt. I'm not moving to Dallas."

Dallas would be the *worst* place for Matt. He seemed to think he was ready, but it was too soon. He needed more time to heal, more time with her.

"Sure you are. There's a really great arts district, and my mom knows a lot of people. She can introduce you to other moms your age. You'll like it."

The first tendrils of alarm unfolded in her stomach. "*You* don't even like Dallas. You said it was oppressive. Do you really think you can go back to real estate, like you're still the same person you used to be?"

The look on his face when he'd been telling Nicola and

Angelo about his family firm—well, he might love his job, but it wasn't going to be the same. He'd walked away because he needed something else.

He needed her.

"I have to be that person. That's the real me. This?" He pointed at the frescoed ceiling. "This is not me. This is some other guy who'd lost his way. Dallas is where I was always trying to get back to. I have you to thank for getting me on the right track."

"Dallas isn't the right track. You're talking about shoe-horning both of us, and a *baby*, into something that doesn't exist anymore. Monte Carlo is the best option for us. We're moving on together. Don't you see?" Desperation laced her words, because it was clear he *didn't* see.

"Monte Carlo is not a place for the mother of my child." His lips firmed into a no-nonsense line she'd never seen before.

"It is when I'm the mother."

Their gazes locked, and the frozen blue of his irises nearly took her breath. All of Matt's incredible depth—the quality she'd always treasured the most—had vanished.

"I don't want you around those kind of people," he said.

"*Those* kind of people?" Her spine stiffened in shock. "And what kind of people would those be, Matt?"

He had the gall to glare at her. "Alcoholics. Like your ex. People who stumble home after a night of who knows what, like Vincenzo, and throw phone parties."

Eyes wide, she snickered to cover her rising distress. "Would you like a stepladder to see over that double standard you just threw up? May I remind you where we met?"

"That's irrelevant. You're not going to Monte Carlo."

Who was this man talking to her out of Matt's mouth and watching her from his eyes, but who clearly was *not* Matt? It was like he'd put on another mask, but this one scared her.

"Are we really on such opposite sides of this? How can that be?" She looked for some glimmer of the empathy they'd always had. It wasn't there, as if the link between them had been severed. The tendril of panic exploded. "I don't understand what's going on."

"We're having a baby. A baby that will be raised in Dallas, where it will have the best care and the best opportunities." The corner he was pushing her into grew sharp against her back. He *never* pushed. Why now? "Where we can have a good life and be happy. Like you said."

Dallas was his idea of a good life? "What, exactly, do you envision me doing in Dallas? Tea parties with your mother?"

He shrugged. "Sure. If you want to. Or volunteer. My sister-in-law runs a women's shelter. Maybe that would appeal to you. It'll take a while to get back in the swing of things, even for me, but I usually get invitations to at least one or two social events a week. Charity balls and the like. When the baby comes, you can take it easy and focus on being a mother."

"Charity balls?" Her voice squeaked. Which would be unremarkable except it was the highest tone she'd accomplished in a very long time. "Have we actually met? Hi, I'm Evangeline La Fleur, and I live in Europe. I'd like for the father of my child to live in Europe with me."

"Or?"

The challenge snaked through her.

"Or don't. But you're talking about a life in Dallas that I can't do." If she put down roots in Dallas, what would happen to her if it didn't work out? If he decided he didn't want her to stay after all?

"Can't? Or won't?" His tone sliced through her, and tears burned at the corners of her eyes.

"Can't." She took a deep, calming breath, but it shuddered in her chest. "Matt, have you listened to me at all? I'd die in that environment. Die, as in wither up into a dried bit of nothing and blow away."

They *both* would. Why was he being so stubborn?

"You'll be with me. I'll keep you entertained." His wolf-ish smile unleashed a nauseous wave in her abdomen.

"Is that all I am to you?"

"No. Of course not." He shook his head, sobering, and every fiber of her being wished for him to follow that with, *I love you.* "I want you to be my wife."

That's when it all snapped into place. The sick churning in her stomach sped up.

"You haven't been trying to get over Amber. That's why it's taking so long. What you've been searching for isn't a cure—you've been looking for a *replacement.* The whole time. And you found one."

"No one can replace Amber." A lethal edge to his expression whipped out and knifed her in a tender place deep inside. "I would never attempt to try."

"Of course. My mistake." One of many. But she couldn't let it go, couldn't stop from ensuring they both heard the brutal truth. "I've been falling in love with you. All along. Tell me that's one-sided."

The harsh lines of his face softened. "I'm sorry. I'm not trying to hurt you."

"But you're going to anyway."

Her heart froze in disbelief. She'd put it out there, only to have it slapped down. It had never occurred to her that she wouldn't be successful at healing him. That the baby wouldn't be the answer. That her feelings wouldn't be returned.

But Matt was honest to a fault, and he'd never lie to her. He didn't love her.

He couldn't, because she wasn't Amber. She'd never be able to fill the empty place in his heart, and she'd been a fool to think that demon could ever be slayed.

Her whole life had been shaped by rejection at the hands of people who didn't love her because she wasn't someone else. She wasn't Lisa. She wasn't Sara Lear. And she *wasn't Amber.*

"Evangeline…" He sighed, and deep lines appeared around his eyes, aging him. "I've never made you any promises. I don't make promises I don't intend to keep. And I'm not ready to be in love again. Might never be."

Brutal. She'd had no idea how severe the truth could really be. "So you're proposing we get married and raise a kid. But as roommates?"

"We've been living together without being in love. Why does being married have to be any different? It'll be like Venice, but permanent. If you don't want to volunteer, then do something else, maybe related to music. Give private singing lessons."

"I can't sing," she choked out, and the final stitch holding her heart together snapped. The organ fell into two pieces somewhere in the vicinity of her womb, where the child she thought they'd love as a couple grew.

"Piano lessons then." He took her hand, squeezing, as if nothing was wrong. As if everything was going to work out fine. "If you taught me, you can teach anyone. It doesn't matter to me as long as the baby is taken care of."

It doesn't matter to me.

She was nothing more than a warm oven for his offspring. Not someone to love and cherish. It was the ultimate rejection of everything she'd imagined their relationship to be.

She yanked her hand out of his grasp.

She'd invented a connection—one that didn't actually exist—out of her own loneliness and fear of an empty future. In the end, Matt wanted something from her far more damaging, and far more heartbreaking, than she could have ever predicted. He wanted her to sacrifice everything that made her who she was, and in return, he vowed to *never* love her the way he loved Amber.

Maybe he wasn't capable of loving anyone other than Amber.

Why hadn't she realized that sooner?

"Oh, the baby will be taken care of. *My* baby," she corrected fiercely. This was one time when she'd be doing the rejecting. "I don't actually need your help, in case that wasn't clear. I'm not a wide-eyed sixteen-year-old, terrified and penniless. I've got a net worth in the eight figures. The baby will have every opportunity available under the sun. You go back to Dallas and attend some stuck-up snobby rich people's charity event. I'll be in Monte Carlo living the life that makes sense for me. *You* can have a relationship with your child through the internet."

She fled up the stairs, tears streaming, and locked herself in the bedroom to finish packing.

Twelve

"Evangeline." Matthew banged on the door again, barely resisting the urge to kick it in. "Open the door. We're not finished, not by a long shot."

What in the name of all that was holy had just happened? Somehow, Evangeline had broken up with him, like they were a real couple.

But weren't they? He was going to marry her. He *wanted* to marry her.

He'd invested considerable energy into figuring out the next steps—marriage, a house, a stake in the ground—and Evangeline was *throwing it back in his face*.

This was killing him. His insides tossed and turned faster than a shoreline in a hurricane.

"Oh, we're finished," she called, and slammed something—a drawer. "A good lawyer will help us work out the visitation rights."

Visitation rights. Lawyers. If this was a nightmare, it was not ending fast enough.

"Lawyers are not the answer."

"Why, don't you have one?"

He rolled his eyes at her scathing tone. "I *am* one.

Granted, not well-versed in the ins and outs of international custody law. But I'm pretty sure I could hold my own given time to acclimate."

Some shuffling. The door flung open to reveal Evangeline's ravaged face. He hated it when she cried. Hated being the reason.

"You're a *lawyer*?" She spit it out like he'd admitted to being a member of the Black Panthers.

But at least she was talking to him again. He had to get this situation back under control before she took off to Monte Carlo and he never heard from her again.

"I passed the bar. Is that really important in light of the other really important thing we should be discussing? The baby?" he prompted.

She crossed her arms. "Well, we're full of disclosures today, aren't we? No wonder you're so sanctimonious. Anything else you forgot to tell me?"

"It's not like I hid it on purpose to make you mad. It just never came up."

"But it perfectly illustrates the point. I *trusted* you." She was so worked up, she bristled. "I've never been anything but honest about who I am yet I don't know you at all."

Direct hit. He had worn his mask far longer than she had.

Punching photographers. Sex on the roof. Midnight confessionals. None of that was really him, and she was calling him on it. This was all his fault.

A doozy of a headache landed right behind his eyeballs.

"I didn't set out to deceive you."

All at once, she deflated. "I thought…well, it doesn't matter now."

"It does matter. Evangeline—" He pressed a fingertip to both eyelids, willing the headache to disappear. It didn't. "I don't want to deal with custody and visitation through lawyers. The baby belongs with both parents."

Evangeline and the baby belonged with him, in Dallas.

Their choices about the future had been taken from them, and he'd think about why that made him so happy later.

"Then come to Monte Carlo with me." Her soft brown eyes beseeched him, pulling at him. Unearthing the confusing, unnatural reaction he had to her. "Prove that you're the man I think you are. More hinges on it than what's going to happen with the baby. You came to me broken. I want you to be whole again. Let me heal you."

"But you've already done that." He couldn't help it. He pulled her into his arms, and the feel of her, the warmth, the familiar scent of her hair, knocked his equilibrium loose, nearly putting him on the ground. "That's why I can go back to Dallas and pick up the reins of who I was. Because you made me feel alive again."

Alive. Yes. And without her, what would he be?

"No." She buried her face in his neck. "You're not healed. If you were, you would be able to love me."

That was the kicker. They had different definitions of *healed.*

"I didn't lie to you. I told you I didn't have anything to give. I'm sorry, but a baby doesn't change that."

She nodded. "I understand. And it doesn't change the fact that I can't marry you. If we were in love, I…well, it doesn't matter, does it?"

She'd sliced through everything, right to the heart of it. She wanted him to love her. And he couldn't.

The purgatory of loss was too painful. He wasn't willing to risk backsliding into a hole of depression again. Not even for her.

Especially for her. She made him feel too much.

This was not the opportune time to figure out all this. He'd been searching for a way to get back on track, not searching for someone like Evangeline.

"No compromise?" He had a sick feeling in his gut that he already knew the answer.

"Oh, Matt." She kissed him, lightly, and her lips lifted

too quickly. "Sure I'd compromise. London. Madrid. Pick a place. Monte Carlo isn't nearly as important as what it represents. You won't fully heal until you accept that your old life is gone. You can't go back. Neither of us can. All we can do is move forward. If that's what you want, Monte Carlo is the answer."

He couldn't chase her around the globe like a teenager with a trust fund and no responsibilities.

"Not for me."

It wasn't the right answer for her, either. She'd never find the next steps in Monte Carlo, and the anguish would swallow her whole if he wasn't around. How in the world did she think she'd survive without him?

The baby belonged with him. *She* belonged with him. He wanted to howl with the injustice of it, that he couldn't make her see the logic.

She stepped out of his embrace, dry-eyed. "Then, this is goodbye."

Matthew called a cab instead of Lucas, though he knew his brother would pick him up from the airport. Family would always be there for him, regardless of the grief he'd put them through for the past eighteen months. But he couldn't face anyone.

Not yet. Not when he still couldn't process that he'd left Evangeline in Venice.

The mother of his child. And he'd had to let her go.

After several more arguments, a bucket of tears—not all hers—and a bunch of slammed doors, he'd finally given up trying to reason with her. Stubborn woman. She refused to see what was best and actually threatened to disappear if he didn't accept her decision.

Ultimately, their connection was nothing but the magic of Venice, blowing smoke and illusion to cover the truth. They weren't meant to be together.

The cab pulled up at his parents' house. The driver hefted

the suitcases from the trunk, accepted the folded bill with a nod and drove off, leaving Matthew on the sidewalk in the middle of the suburban neighborhood he'd grown up in. The neighborhood he didn't recognize at all.

His mother had planted something flowery and purple in the side yard that he'd never seen before, and the house's wood trim had been painted. Maybe the brick had been power-washed. A car rushed by on the street behind him, likely only driving thirty miles an hour, but it felt more like a hundred. All of it lent to the sense of being somewhere unfamiliar.

There weren't any cars in Venice. Boats slipped by quietly in the canal or sometimes the cheerful call of a gondolier announced its presence. People strolled the streets and enjoyed a slower pace. He'd grown used to it. Preferred it.

The front door creaked, and his mother poked her blond head out. "Now there's a sight for sore eyes. Get in here, honey. You should have told me you were coming."

Matthew grinned at the break in her voice. "Hey, Mama. It was a surprise."

"It certainly is. Surprise me less or you'll give me a heart attack." She flew over the doorstep and into a fierce hug.

This, at least, felt very familiar. Very welcoming. He'd missed her.

Mama hustled him into the house and fluttered around, doing a bang-up job of ignoring Matthew's protests about staying in a hotel. To stem the tide, he carried his stuff to the extra bedroom upstairs. Arguing with Mama did not ever end well.

"Sit. Let me look at you." Mama sank onto the couch and he followed. She smoothed a lock of hair from his forehead. "Staying long?"

"Yeah." He knew what she was really asking. "I'm home for good."

That put weight on his shoulders. He'd thought he was

ready. He *was* ready. But it was so permanent. And so Evangeline-free.

Her sharp gaze swept him, twice, with a combination of disbelief and hope. "Did you find what you were looking for?"

The harsh laugh scraped at his throat. "Not really. But I figured out it's because I didn't actually know what I was looking for. I don't do well without a plan."

"You never have. So what's your plan now?"

"I'm going back to WFP. Lucas has managed to get himself into a hole, and I'm going to get him out." First time in a long time he had a sense of purpose. A goal. It felt good. Right.

Mama shot him a puzzled glance. "A hole? Did he tell you that?"

"I know about Richards Group. It's partly the reason I came home." The other part had everything to do with a singular desire to be dependable, straight-arrow Matthew Wheeler again. To do something he excelled at and had ultimate control over.

"I think you should talk to him. We'll have a big family dinner to celebrate you being home. Call your brother. Tell him to come early so you can get on the same page." She smiled. "Far be it from me to get in the middle of my boys, but honey, you left. Lucas has been handling things. I doubt he's going to take kindly to you sticking your nose into WFP and bossing him around. A word to the wise."

Matthew checked the eye-roll out of sheer respect for the woman who had birthed him. But it was hard.

"I'm not going to boss him around, Mama. I'm here to help."

She nodded. "Just you remember that. You're helping. Not in charge."

The transatlantic flight caught up to him then, and he cracked his jaw with a yawn. "I'm going to take a shower and maybe watch TV for a couple of mindless hours." Decompress. Be alone without his mother's shrewd gaze on him. He pulled her into a long hug. "Thanks. For letting me come home."

"Silly." She thumped his shoulder, her eyes shiny and full. "You're still my kid, no matter how big you get. I love you. You're always welcome here."

He almost spilled everything then, all the heartache of the past eighteen months, the depression, the disorientation. How he'd experienced it again tenfold on the flight home at the hands of a different woman. But the wounds of Evangeline were far too fresh and the wounds of Amber far too…faded.

He frowned. When had that happened?

"See you at dinner."

Dropping a kiss on his mother's cheek, he went upstairs to clear his mind with a hot shower, which didn't work.

When he'd last been in Dallas, the burden of grief had turned the sunniest of days dark. Amber was constantly on his mind, how he couldn't go on without her. How everything they'd planned was dashed. He'd expected coming home to bring all that back. It hadn't.

When he thought about Amber now, it was with a hazy sort of warm rush. The prongs of grief had lifted.

The skin he washed was the same. But the man inside wasn't. That's why the neighborhood and his mother's house had been unrecognizable. Despite all his yearning to slip back in time, to a place where he knew everything was safe and right, he couldn't. The only thing he could do was accept that he had changed.

Like Evangeline had said.

But if he accepted that his life was something different now, who would he be?

He called Lucas and then flipped on the TV to lose himself in the oblivion of sleep.

The door crashed against the wall, waking him. Groggily, he sat up and swung his legs off the edge of the bed. The empty bed.

He wasn't in Venice with Evangeline. He was in Dallas. Alone.

A fuzzy Lucas lounged against the door frame, hand in his pants' pocket and a smirk on his face.

"God Almighty, you look like roadkill in August." Lucas tsked.

"Thanks. That's exactly what I needed to hear. I was sleeping, by the way," Matthew groused and rubbed a hand across his eyes. His brother's form snapped into focus. "Though I appreciate that you were so eager to see me you couldn't wait."

Lucas snorted out a laugh. "I just didn't believe you were actually here. Had to see it for myself. You back?"

"Looks that way."

"All the way back?"

"Why does everyone keep asking me that? I'm here, aren't I?"

Lucas sat on the edge of the bed a couple feet away, dipping the mattress. "You were in bad shape. I'm concerned. Sue me."

Well, I am a sanctimonious lawyer.

Matthew's head dropped into his hands. It wasn't just jet lag crushing him. Evangeline—knowing he'd hurt her, being without her—weighed more than he could bear.

"Honestly, I don't know if 'all the way back' is possible."

"Amber's death nearly destroyed you. Don't let it finish the job," Lucas advised quietly. "You took some time away. Now rejoin life. I'm working on trouncing Richards Group. Another Wheeler on the job can't hurt."

Matthew nearly laughed. "If only Amber were the problem, I'd be all set. Unfortunately, I traded one impossible-to-solve issue for another."

Lucas nodded sagely. "This has to do with the very sexy lady you met. What happened?"

Matthew met his brother's sharp gaze. "How do you know about that?"

"Everyone knows about that. You photograph well, as it happens. So she figured out she's too good for you, huh? Am I going to be nursing you through a broken heart?"

Matthew growled. "Shut up. You don't know what you're talking about."

"Oh, poor baby. Did she make you cry?" Lucas thumped him on the arm, and Matthew shot him a glare.

"Back off. She's pregnant."

He hadn't meant to say anything. But it came out nonetheless, too huge to stay under wraps.

"Then what are you doing here without her?" His brother's eyes narrowed. "Oh. It's not yours."

Matthew's fist curled, and he almost let it fly, but curbed the impulse at the last second. Where had that anger come from? He wasn't in Venice, free to do whatever he wanted, when he wanted to.

"Of course it's mine. And God, it's a mess."

Lucas started laughing and didn't stop even when Matthew shoved him. Finally, Lucas wiped his eyes. "Oh, how the mighty have fallen."

"What's that supposed to mean?" His brother's face might actually be improved with a good slug to the jaw.

Still sniggering, Lucas crossed his arms. "May I remind you of what you said to me about Cia? I believe you accused me of getting a one-night stand pregnant and self-righteously informed me that accidents happen."

His stomach twisted as he vaguely recalled saying something asinine to that effect. "Is it too late to apologize?"

"Nah." Lucas grinned. "No apology needed. It's nice to know you're human like the rest of us. Where is she now? Did you have a fight or something?"

"Worse. She threw my marriage proposal back in my face and took off with her friends."

"That sucks." Lucas whistled in disbelief. "Women. Can't live with 'em, can't shoot 'em."

Matthew had made it sound like Evangeline was a flighty, irresponsible girl who didn't understand what she'd given up, which was completely unfair and not representative of how badly the whole thing had gone down.

"I guess I didn't actually propose."

Lucas's eyebrows rose. "What did you do then?"

"Told her we were getting married." Out loud, it sounded even worse than it did in his head. "It made sense, you know? You marry a woman you get pregnant. Instead, she's talking about lawyers and custody arrangements."

"Geez, are you that clueless?" Lucas huffed out a disgusted breath. "No wonder she dumped you. You don't have a romantic bone in your body, obviously. How in the world did *you* score with Eva?"

That bristled the hair on the back of Matthew's neck. "I didn't *score* with her. It wasn't like that. We had something—" *Special. Meaningful. Unexplainable.* "I don't know. Different."

"Different than what? Amber?"

Matthew's throat burned, and he almost used it as an excuse to clam up. But once, he and Lucas had been close. That their bond had deteriorated was totally his fault. He wanted it back. And the first step was being honest.

"Different than anything I've ever experienced. Amber fit me, fit my plans. Evangeline…doesn't."

But she fit Matt comfortably, like a second skin. Evangeline *was* different—sexy, arousing, provoking and flat-out frightening.

"So? Life is what happens when you're making other plans."

If only it was that easy.

"Since you're so smart, you tell me. If everything you thought you knew about yourself got flipped upside down, what would you do?" Yeah, asking *what would Lucas do* had gotten him into this mess. Why break tradition?

A perceptive light crept into his brother's eyes. "Well, now. That very thing happened, as a matter of fact. When it did, I looked to my older brother and said, *that's who I want to be*."

Matthew flinched. "Me? Which part of dumping all my responsibilities in your lap did you aim to replicate?"

"Nobody blames you for that. You needed a break. But I guess you forgot the rest of that conversation the afternoon Grandpa died. You said I could be you, and you were going to go be me. I took that seriously. I stepped up because I wanted to be as successful as you."

"I took it seriously, too." Matthew had to chuckle at the irony. "You want to know how I got Evangeline's attention? I pretended I was you. It worked."

Lucas grinned. "I've never seduced a pop star."

"Neither have I. I didn't know that's who she was at the time. All I wanted was to feel something again." And he'd done a stellar job. He felt stupid, frustrated and out of his element. "Then bam! There she was, like an answer to a prayer, only I hadn't prayed for *that*. I didn't have any idea what to do with her."

"Well, you must have had *some* idea since she's, you know, pregnant." Lucas ducked, but Matthew hadn't been planning to smack him. Not right this minute, anyway.

"Yeah, I'm not going to kiss and tell. Hope you get over your disappointment real soon." He flopped back against the pillow, exhausted. "Now she doesn't want anything to do with me, and my kid is going to be living in Europe while I'm here. Mama is going to be so disappointed."

"Mama? What about you? Aren't you disappointed in yourself?"

"I didn't need you to point that out."

Of course he was disappointed. He'd dreamed of a family for a long time. Instantly, the image of Evangeline holding his child, her beautiful face luminous as she smiled at the bundle, popped into his mind, and the sharp stab to the gut nearly doubled him over.

"I don't know what to do."

"You're going to figure it out." Lucas put a brotherly hand on Matthew's shoulder. "I've never seen you fail at something you put your heart into."

He eyed his little brother with new respect. Lucas had stepped into the role Matthew formerly occupied, and with more success than probably anyone had expected, thanks in no small part to Cia. Never underestimate the power of the right woman.

Lucas excused himself so Matthew could get ready for dinner.

When he arrived downstairs, everyone was already at the table. Conversation ground to a sudden halt—obviously because they'd been discussing him—when he came into view.

"Hey, son." His dad, who looked tan and fit, jumped up to give him a brief manly hug.

"Playing a lot of golf lately?"

His dad nodded. "Lucas is running the show at WFP, and I'm enjoying life. Care for a round?"

Matthew agreed without really intending to, but he was home. Home meant doing all the things he used to. Might as well reestablish the routine right away.

Cia glanced up at him and flicked her long, dark hair from her shoulder. "You'll forgive me if I don't get up." She pointed to her huge stomach, and he quickly averted his eyes. Pregnancy was a sore subject.

"Cia."

He kissed his sister-in-law's cheek and smiled at Mama, then proceeded to suffer through a long discussion about the strategies Lucas was working to drive Richards Group back to Houston where their competitor belonged. It was staggering to hear Lucas spit out such cogent, well-thought-out plans.

More than once, his attention wandered back to Venice, only to snap back to the present when someone said his name. *Matthew.* He'd been called that more times today alone than in all of the past few months.

It felt weird to answer to it.

Afterward, he flopped into one of the wicker chairs on Mama's porch, across from Lucas and Cia. They giggled and nuzzled each other until he thought he'd throw up.

"Get a room."

"Hey, just because you screwed things up with your woman doesn't mean I can't enjoy mine." Lucas ducked as Cia smacked him.

"Leave him alone," she said with a conciliatory kiss to her husband's jaw.

Matthew did a double take. His sister-in-law had never liked him. "Defending me? What is the world coming to?"

But she shot him a mellow smile instead of flaying him alive like she'd have done in the past. "You tell me. What has your world come to, Matthew?"

"Disaster," he muttered. Louder, he said, "Lucas spill all my beans?"

"No, the internet did. It was quite the discussion at the shelter for a week. Did you at least come home with an autograph or two?"

Yeah. Evangeline had taken a Sharpie to his insides all right.

Matthew grimaced. "I came home with nothing."

"I see your attitude hasn't improved. Shame." Cia clucked. "Now I owe Lucas something that's going to be very hard for me to do in my current state."

The smoldering glance she skewered his brother with said she'd figure out a way to pay up or die trying. They seemed blissfully happy, even almost a year into their marriage. Who would have thought?

"Did you lose a bet?"

"Yeah." Lucas answered for her. "The second she saw

the pictures of you and Eva, she swore you'd never come home. So I won."

Matthew shook his head. "I don't know how you could make such a bet over a picture."

Coolly, Cia evaluated him. "You haven't seen them. Have you?" Without waiting for his answer, she held out a hand to Lucas. "Phone, please."

When she got it, she tapped a few times and handed it to Matthew. Pulse hammering, he glanced at the photo taken in front of the restaurant in Venice, and zeroed in on Evangeline's beautiful, radiant face. The small resolution didn't diminish her light in the slightest. She burst from the screen, burst into his gut. The reporter he'd punched took a great picture.

"That picture is the first evidence I've seen that you have teeth. You have a nice smile," Cia said quietly.

He tore his gaze off the woman in the photo to look at the guy she was with. Him. But a version of Matthew Wheeler he'd never seen before.

"Before you left," Cia continued, "you had a permanent scowl. Kind of like now."

He certainly didn't have a scowl on his face in the picture. He looked happy. Blissful even, with his arm around Evangeline. They were close, so close, as if they couldn't bear to be apart for the few moments it took to reach the street. Her face turned up toward his, ignoring the iconic scenery around her. They looked like a couple. A real couple.

A couple so in love they only saw each other.

Whether he wanted it or not, it had happened. He'd been falling in love with Evangeline all along.

Lucas jumped in with a spectacular double-team. "That's the smile of a man who's a goner. If you're so miserable without her, why aren't you wherever she is, making it right?"

His brother—the relationship expert. Matthew almost rolled his eyes. "We're too different to make it work."

A lie. He was too afraid to make it work. He'd come home because running away was what he did. His eyelids slammed shut. Was that really who he'd become? A quitter?

"That's pure BS. You're not trying to make it work. You're here, and she's there. Trust me when I say pride won't keep you warm at night. Swallow yours. And watch a You Tube video on how to propose properly to a woman."

Maybe his brother *had* learned a thing or two about what it took. As he reevaluated Lucas with his arm around his pregnant wife, Matthew had a nasty epiphany. Lucas wasn't a screwup, or even much of a womanizer. In trying to be Lucas, he'd been chasing a shadow that didn't exist.

He hadn't been acting like his brother—he'd been Matthew Wheeler all along, but a better, braver, bolder version, who went by the name of Matt. Evangeline had tapped into his secret longings, ripped off his "Matthew" mask and enabled him to discover who he really was underneath the name.

The man Amber married had vanished and become someone else—a man in love with the mother of his child. An ocean separated them because he'd been blindly, selfishly hanging on to slim threads of the past, too afraid of descending into depression again to realize he'd lost everything important.

He wanted to be that guy who kept up with Evangeline La Fleur and had sex on the roof and believed in the whims of fate that had seen fit to blow her into his path. He wanted to be with her and their child, regardless of whether it happened according to his plan.

The Screwup hat was firmly on Matthew's head. But the mistake hadn't been the accidental pregnancy—it had been letting Evangeline go.

How in the world could he make that right?

Thirteen

Evangeline lay on the bed and wiped her eyes for the fortieth time. Morning sickness was worse than a slow death at the hands of sadistic monkeys. Crackers didn't help. Ginger ale didn't help. Cursing Matt didn't help and usually made her cry. Like now.

She craved his egg-white omelets with every pregnancy hormone in her body. All the other hormones craved him.

How could she still be so torn apart over a man who'd stripped her down to her base layer and then *rejected* her? She'd taken a huge leap of faith and trusted him enough to fall in love, only to be crushed. Again.

Really, she couldn't be angry with him. He hadn't lied to her. She'd been lying to herself about what he needed. He'd rather suffer than get over Amber.

But she *was* angry. And devastated. So much so, she couldn't stand to be around him any longer. The look on his face when she'd threatened to disappear had nearly killed her, but what else could she do?

Vincenzo's cousin, Nicola, knocked on the open door. "You need something, *cara*?"

"Thanks. I'm okay." She wasn't but Nicola didn't have

any magic capable of fixing her broken heart. Thank God she'd come to Monte Carlo, where people understood her.

"We go to a club soon. VIP lounge. No paparazzi. You join us?" The elfin woman raised a brow. "Maybe you meet someone new who helps you forget."

Ha. If only. "I better pass. I doubt someone new would care too much for me running to the bathroom every five minutes."

The effort required to simply get dressed was enough of a deterrent to a night out. Then there were the smoke machines, which probably pumped out fumes toxic to a baby. Flashing lights were guaranteed to give her a headache. Cocktails would flow—watered down most likely, but with enough alcohol to render them off-limits.

Of course all of that was just noise. She missed Matt, missed Venice, and nothing else held much appeal.

Nicola nodded and left her alone.

Evangeline bit back an urge to call after her, to beg her to come back and sit awhile. But Evangeline didn't want to be a burden on her nonpregnant friends. Which was all of them.

Still, Monte Carlo was beautiful. Outside the window of her room in Nicola's high-rise condo, the city unfolded in a myriad of lights, energy and people, generating an exciting vibe that spilled out into the Mediterranean via the hundreds of yachts lining the shore.

Alone time was good. She'd come here to feed her newly awakened muse. Now she had plenty of time to see what new brilliance flowed from her fingers.

But instead of reaching for the paper and pen on her bedside table—which had sat untouched for two days—she retrieved the printed page from under her pillow and unfolded the song she'd written in Venice the night she'd fallen asleep on the couch.

She'd probably read these words a hundred times now. The theme of connection ran through every line. Of course, because she craved it. Losing her voice had been devastating because it was the link between her and the listener.

But the song spoke to a different kind of connection. One between people, but deeper than the superficial link between a singer and a fan. It was about bonds, family. Things she'd never had at any point in her life, but somehow the right expression had come from her soul.

Because Matt's soul spilled over into hers with his strong sense of unity, goodness…and now she was crying again. How could she have gleaned so much from his depths when he'd closed himself off? It shouldn't be possible. But the evidence was on the page.

It was definitely a good thing she couldn't sing this. She'd never get through the whole thing without breaking down. Sara Lear would do the song justice, and it would be a nice hit for her already-stellar career.

Why couldn't she imagine Sara singing it? Professional jealousy? Probably.

She read the words again. She had to let go. This was part of moving on, something she must find the strength to do. Her voice was gone, but she had a baby on the way. One day, she'd like to look her child in the face and be able to say *I overcame a huge struggle. You can, too.*

One day, she'd like to tell Matt how he'd helped her realize she was more than just a voice, more than Eva. She still had something of value to give.

The song was proof.

All at once, she knew why she couldn't imagine Sara Lear singing this song. Sara didn't need a hit song writer— she had plenty of those barking at her door. Evangeline hadn't written this song for Sara, but for someone else entirely.

And now was the right time to give it away.

Before she could change her mind, she picked up her phone and dialed. "It's Evangeline. Your sister."

Family.

What had started as a simple phone call was actually much more profound. Her heart hadn't just been opened to Matt, but to a whole new world of connection. Even though he'd devastated her, he'd also introduced the wonders of permanence, longevity—all only possible if she allowed roots to grow.

"Hi." Lisa's surprise came through the line clearly in the one short word.

"Sorry to call you with no warning." How did you build a relationship from scratch? Start slowly or jump in with both feet? "I've been going through a tough time and I wanted to apologize for losing touch. Can we start over?"

Maybe somewhere in the middle, then.

"I'd like that. How are you? Your voice is different."

Evangeline chuckled. "The surgery messed it up. Listen, I wanted to ask you. Are you still singing?"

"Yeah. At school, we have a vocal group. I do that and karaoke on the weekends. Nothing that's going to get me noticed, but Dad said I can record some demos after graduation."

Dad. Her stomach twisted at the label Lisa so easily gave the man who'd done nothing more for Evangeline than donate sperm. But this was part of letting go too, and nurturing those fledgling roots instead of chopping them off at the source.

"I have a better idea. I wrote a song for you. I'd like to hear you sing it, and then if we both agree it's everything I hope, I'll book you a recording session with my former producer. He'll lay it down right."

"Omigod. Are you serious?" Half of Lisa's sentence came out a squeal. "You wrote a song for me? Why?"

A million different throwaway responses rose up, but this was about forging a new direction and exposing the deepest parts of herself. About living up to the bravery Matt had seen in her.

"I'm branching into a new career. As a songwriter. I expect I'll write quite a few songs. Who better to write for than family? If we work really hard and are fully committed, the partnership can launch both of our careers."

Committed. It had a nice ring to it. She'd had precious little commitment to anything and expected it to drop a weight on her chest. But instead, the idea of collaborating with her sister, long term, carried the most intense sense of peace.

Best of all, if someone asked her, *What are you going to do now that you can't sing anymore?*, she had an answer.

A new direction as a songwriter and a new direction with family. Timely, since she was going to have a family of her own when the baby was born.

A wave of guilt clogged her throat. She'd deliberately ensured that family would only consist of two—her and the baby.

That wasn't fair to Matt, Matt's family or the baby.

Evangeline surprised herself by saying, "I'm planning to be in the States soon. Would you mind if I dropped by Detroit so we can work this song face-to-face?"

"That would be killer. When?"

"I'm not sure exactly. I'll call you. I have a stop to make first. In Dallas."

Matt didn't love her—and she'd almost accepted that—but she didn't want her child to grow up without knowing its family. Her baby deserved to know his or her father. Grandparents. Uncle and aunts. Her child wouldn't have to suffer crushing loneliness its whole life. Like she had.

But none of that was going to happen if she hid in Europe forever.

Pregnancy hormones, or maybe just sheer disappointment in herself and in Matt for not being what she wanted, had driven her to make a rash decision she now regretted. What else had she categorically rejected before it could reject her?

She had to figure out a way to be a coparent with Matt, no matter how much he'd hurt her. Her baby needed her to be brave. She had to go to Dallas and forge a relationship with her child's family. She and Matt *were* getting a family together; it just wasn't going to happen the way she'd have liked. Somehow, she'd make it work, no matter where she ended up living.

The flight to Dallas was miserable. Two layovers, one delayed flight and a near-morning-sickness-mishap in the aisle of first class later, Evangeline plunked down in a cab and handed the driver Francis and Andrew Wheeler's address. When Matt had shoved it at her with instructions to mail any legal documents to his attention there, she'd never expected to use it personally.

When the cab stopped, her breath caught. The Wheelers' house was exactly what she'd envisioned. Welcoming. Homey. Located in a quiet, stately neighborhood she'd have no problem allowing the baby to run free through.

A pretty middle-aged woman answered her knock. Matt had inherited his mother's blue eyes and blond hair. The older woman's shocked gaze reminded her an awful lot of Matt's face when she'd handed him the pregnancy test.

"Hello," Evangeline said. "We haven't met but—"

"Matthew's not here."

"Oh. You recognize me." That had not been the greeting she'd expected. Actually, she hadn't known what to expect.

"Of course. You're the mother of my grandchild."

Not Eva. Not Evangeline. But something else entirely— part of a family. She took it as a sign that she'd made the right decision in coming here.

"I am."

Obviously Matt had told everyone about the baby.

Matt's mother blinked and her smile warmed. "And I'm terribly rude. I'm Fran. Please come in. You must be exhausted from your flight. May I call you Evangeline? I'm very happy to meet you."

Fran ushered her inside, chattering as if they'd met years

ago instead of minutes. The Wheeler household engulfed her the moment she stepped into the foyer. Warm, rich creams and teals tastefully accented the formal living room, but it didn't feel stuffy. Framed photographs lined the mantel of a large fireplace. All the pictures contained smiling people, clustered together as if they couldn't get close enough.

A family lived here.

"Your home is beautiful. I see where Matt gets his taste."

The older woman shot her a puzzled glance. "Thank you. You call him Matt? And he lets you?"

"Is that unusual?" Evangeline perched on the edge of the sofa and Fran joined her.

"He hates that nickname. Always has. Says it sounds too much like a frat boy with a skateboard under his arm." Fran patted her arm. "I like you already. Anyone who can unstarch my son is a friend of mine."

Matt starched? Evangeline laughed involuntarily. If only Fran knew how unstarched her son could truly be.

"I hope we can be friends. I'm actually glad Matt's not here. I came to see you."

"You did?"

She had no idea how much Matt had told his parents, but the relationship between her and Fran could and should last a very long time.

"I did a selfish thing by taking off to Monte Carlo. Matt hurt me, and I used that as an excuse to keep everyone away from my baby. But I want you, and all of Matt's family, to be a part of the baby's life. It's very important to me."

Fran's eyes lit up, just like Matt's did when he was happy. "I'd like that, too. I'd like it better if my grandchild's parents were married. But I promise that's all I'll say to interfere with what my son has clearly informed me is not my business."

So maybe he had told her everything. Having that kind of bond with a mother—she couldn't fathom it. This woman had shaped Matt, instilling in him many wonderful qualities. And most of them were outside of the kitchen. His depth, his sense of commitment, his patience and kindness. All products of his relationship with his family.

Having roots allowed for magnificent things to grow. She wanted that for her baby, but recognized that *she* had to make it happen by sticking around and creating the connections. Maybe she'd open herself to being hurt. And maybe this family would welcome her.

"Marriage was one of the many areas where we disagreed," Evangeline admitted readily. "But I'm here because I realized I was wrong about a few of them. For example, I'm willing to reevaluate my stance on living in Europe."

"Well, that's a relief. It's a shame Matthew's not here so you can tell him personally. I think he'd be very interested in where else you might compromise. Ironically, you just missed him."

She should talk to Matt. No matter how hard it might be. They were going to be parents, whether she wished they could be more or not.

"Do you mind if I wait?"

Fran smiled. "You might be waiting a long time. He flew to Monte Carlo this morning."

Apparently Matthew *was* going to chase Evangeline around the globe.

He'd done everything short of walking up and down Rue Grimaldi yelling Evangeline's name in order to find her. Vincenzo hadn't realized she'd left Monte Carlo, and his cousin shook her head and said, "Sorry, *cara*. She said *ciao* and nothing else."

Frustrated and quite sick of airports, Matthew slumped against the seat of the final vehicle in a long series of shuttles from place to place to place—a water taxi. He needed to regroup, and what better place to figure out what the hell he was doing than Venice?

Palazzo D'Inverno provided the only bit of sanity he'd experienced in forever.

Matthew tipped the driver and clambered up the dock to the water entrance of his house. The palazzo was the only permanent thing in his life, the only thing he actually owned. Coming here had been a gamble. Evangeline had infiltrated this house, and the memories were likely to be vicious.

When he swung open the door, the quiet hush of peace washed over him. Everything was exactly as he'd left it. The piano stood silently in the corner, draped for protection against lack of use. The U of couches faced the balcony overlooking the Grand Canal. Frescos kept watch from the ceiling, the scenes frozen in time for eternity.

The sense of freedom, as if he could do or be anything he wanted was exactly the same, too.

But that probably had to do with the woman standing by the glass, framed by the grandeur of Venice.

"I was starting to think you'd never get here," Evangeline said, and smiled, punching him straight in the gut. Like always.

Evangeline was in Venice. Inside Palazzo D'Inverno, filling his house with her light. What did that smile mean? Was she buttering him up before she handed over the papers detailing the custody arrangement she hoped to talk him into?

"What are you doing here?"

It was far less than he'd like to say. But far more than his suddenly tight throat should have been able to voice.

"Vincenzo caught me at Heathrow. I changed my connecting flight and voila. Here I am."

Which told him not one blessed thing about her intentions. He hated not knowing exactly where she'd been, where she wanted to go, what she was planning, what she was feeling. Once, he would have known instinctively, would have gleaned a hundred nuances from the vibe between them without a word exchanged.

He missed it. He wanted it back.

"How did you know this was where I would end up?"

His voice broke. She was beautiful—radiant like the Madonna with child. Like Evangeline with his child. There was nothing in Dallas, nothing anywhere in the world worth more. Exactly how stupid was he for not realizing that before screwing up everything?

Was she still in love with him? Or had he ruined that, too?

His stomach pitched. Well, he'd just have to convince her to forgive him for being such a shortsighted moron. Negotiation was his best skill.

She shrugged and crossed the room, stopping short of invading his space, likely because he'd given no indication of whether he'd welcome her. "Lucky guess."

Or maybe something else had whispered his destination to her, something unexplainable and incomprehensible. But still real.

"I was coming to you. In Monte Carlo," he said.

"I know. Your mother told me."

Matthew shook his head. Evangeline scrambled his wits. "My mother?"

"I went to Dallas." Her eyes filled. "Matt, I don't want to cut our baby off from you. Or from your family. I was selfish and stupid. Apologies were in order, all the way around, starting with your mother. Ending with you. I'm sorry. I want you to have a relationship with our baby that's more than holidays and birthday cards once a year."

"Oh." Disappointment wrenched his battered heart. What had he expected, that she'd miraculously decided to give him another chance when he'd plainly told her he had nothing to give? "I'm the one who should apologize. I'm sorry, too. So how do you envision a relationship between me and the baby if you're living in Europe?"

"I'm not going to live in Europe. I called my sister. We talked, and she's going to record some songs that I wrote. I never liked the idea of giving my words to Sara Lear. But

Lisa, that's a different story. It'll be a great partnership. I'm going to stay in the States so we can work together."

Pride filled him. She'd found her way after all. "That's fantastic. Why did you fly all the way to Dallas to apologize in person?"

"Well, I was planning to go from Dallas to Detroit. It made sense in the mixed-up files of my pregnant brain."

He contemplated her slight form. "But you're here. Not Detroit."

"A funny thing happened when I got to Dallas. You weren't there. You went to Monte Carlo. I have to know why."

"Evangeline…" He hesitated, unsure how to undo all the damage he'd done the first time by trying to follow rules that made no sense for the man he'd become. But there were no rules in Palazzo D'Inverno. So he said what was in his heart.

"When I got to Dallas, it took about five minutes to know I was still in the valley. And when I looked up, I realized I couldn't get to the top of the mountain unless I had someone with wings to fly me there."

"Me?" she whispered.

He nodded. "Please, please forgive me for all the stupid things I said before. I can't be me without you. I love you."

Tears streamed down her face. "Really?"

"Really." He bridged the gap, drawing her into his arms, and she fell against him, clutching at his shoulders. Warm, light-filled Evangeline was in his arms. "I was the selfish one. Clinging to the past when I had the future right here the whole time."

"I don't understand. You said you weren't ready for that."

"I'm not." Who could ever be ready for someone uninhibited, wild and perfect like Evangeline? "To compensate, I refused to put myself in the position of letting my emotions get the better of me again. The problem with that, of course, is that it was too late. I was already in love with you."

The denial burst from her and he closed her lips with his fingertip.

"Shh. It's true. Amber was an integral part of my life for a long time, and when she died, it was like a car losing an engine. One can't function without the other. But I was never a car to you, and because of that, we fit differently. I couldn't see that until I went home and tried to be a car again."

"Are you saying you don't want to be a car anymore? Or are you trying to talk me into buying one?"

He laughed, shocked at the quaver in it. "I'm saying you were right. I can't pick up the reins of my old life and I don't want to. I want to find a new direction with you and our baby. Wherever the wind blows us. I went to Monte Carlo to tell you that."

Hope spread across her face.

"I want to believe you," she said cautiously. "But I trusted you, and you smashed my heart all to pieces. I can't be a replacement for your wife. How do I know you're really over her?"

"I don't want a replacement. Amber was only one color, and that was right for me before. You're all the colors of the rainbow. It's tattooed on you permanently because that's who you'll always be to me."

Her eyelids dropped for a beat, and when she opened them again, the soft brown sucked him under. "How do you always know the right thing to say?"

Because he'd learned that the right thing had context. The right thing wasn't always the same from day to day, and sometimes you had to do what was right for the person you were at that moment.

He grinned. "Several transatlantic flights in a row give you lots of time to think."

"What do you want? Did you come loaded down with a ring and a fancy marriage proposal?"

The pain in her voice tried and convicted him. He'd hurt

her, and saying the right thing wasn't nearly enough to make up for it.

"No." He'd gone against the very fiber of his being and come here empty-handed. "This time we're doing things according to your schedule. I'll follow you wherever you go, whether we've got a piece of paper calling us husband and wife or not. I will never again utter the word *marriage* until you flat out say that's what you want."

"Your mother will be upset."

Obviously Mama had treated Evangeline to an earful of the Fran Wheeler Sermon on the Merits of Marriage. Hopefully it hadn't stacked up Evangeline's disfavor against him any higher.

"She'll get over it. This is about us and what we want."

"And you don't want to marry me."

"On the contrary. Nothing would make me happier than to claim you as my wife before God and everybody. But it's your choice. Our relationship will be how you define it."

Amber had been his wife; that role fit her and what they'd shared. Evangeline was something else and fit the man he was now. The harder he tried to pin her down, the harder she'd flap her wings to escape. And he wanted her to be free to fly, as long as she waited for him to catch up.

A shrewd glint in her eye set off a frisson of nerves. "What if I wanted to live in Dallas? What would you say?"

"I'd say who are you, and what have you done with the woman I love?"

Her gravelly laugh clawed through his stomach with heat he'd missed. "My name is Evangeline La Fleur. And your name is?"

The best question of all and the easiest to answer. "Matt. My name is Matt."

"Nice to meet you, Matt." She shook his hand solemnly. "That's a nice name. I like it. You know the funny thing about names? They change. You think you're this person, the one the name refers to, and then all of a sudden, you have to redefine yourself."

"And with it comes a new name," he said.

That ripple of understanding passed between them, as strong as it had from the first. Finally, finally, the knot of tension at the base of his skull unwound, and he started to believe he'd leave the valley and crest the mountain with her by his side after all.

"So," he continued. "I'm getting a picture in my head of you living in Dallas. What else should I add to this picture? Will you be living by yourself? Or might I convince you to stay with me?"

A deep smile spread across her face. "You're pretty good at convincing me to stay. I'll give you that. If I stay with you, do I get my own room?"

"Nope. The baby gets his or her own room, but you have to share with me, whether we have a marriage license or not. See, I don't need a replacement wife, but I do need a lover. I seem to have an addiction to inventive positions. And locations, apparently, because I'm envisioning a very sturdy table in the kitchen. And maybe a screened-in porch. A large shower is a must, as well. Sound like something you might consider?"

Say yes. He'd be happy to throw in some begging if it turned the tide.

She shook her head. "You're crazy. I like that."

Crazy. Yes, he was. But only because he'd fallen in love with a woman who allowed him to be and feel and do whatever he wanted.

"Please tell me I haven't totally screwed up things between us. I'm open to discussion on how we'll raise the baby, and I don't care where we live. We can stay here in Venice if you want. I love you and want to be with you the rest of my life, wherever you are, whether we have a marriage license or not."

Her eyes grew misty. "That was the most romantic non-proposal I've ever heard."

"Is that a yes?"

"Not yet. I wasn't done with my apology. I'm sorry I was so stubborn. Before. I never should have tried to force you to heal my way or discounted the idea of living where you wanted to. I've been pretty selfish for a long time, excusing it because I'd lost something important. Important, but not crucial. I can't sing but I haven't lost my voice."

"Of course you haven't. You're *my* voice. You articulate the things in my soul far better than I could."

"Geez." Her lids flew closed and she swallowed heavily. When she met his gaze once more, the powerful connection swept through him again. "I was already going to say yes. But if you want to say some more romantic things, I'm all ears."

His heart took flight. "You were? What swayed you, the sturdy kitchen table or me finally gathering enough wits to tell you I love you?"

"The fact that you flew to Monte Carlo. The rest was nice to hear, though. I came to Venice to tell you I wasn't letting you go again, by the way."

He couldn't help but laugh. They'd chased each other around the globe. "I told you, I'll follow you anywhere."

"Then start walking." She turned and flounced up the stairs, hips swinging saucily. Halfway up, she called over her shoulder, "I'll be naked on the bed, thinking about how much I love you. I'm dying to see what you're going to do first."

Matt was pretty curious too and raced up the stairs to find out what two healed souls could become to each other.

Epilogue

Evangeline shoved the Murano glass bowl directly into the center of the art niche outside the baby's room. Much better. Decorating the home she and Matt had bought—together—down the street from his parents' turned out to be the most fun she'd ever had. Who knew?

Fran came out of the nursery. "Carlos tacked up the border. Do you want to check out the placement before I have him glue it down?"

Matt's mother had taken on the role of Contractor Supervisor and ruled the workers with an iron fist covered in lace. The two women became friends instantly, and Evangeline fell into the habit of consulting the older woman on just about everything. Fran knew color and style and had fantastic taste.

Since Evangeline had never created a home from scratch, the partnership worked beautifully—as long as neither of them mentioned the word *marriage*. She and Fran had politely agreed to disagree about the status of Evangeline's relationship with Matt.

"I'm sure the border is fine, but I do want to see it." Evangeline stepped into the explosion of red, white and blue, the color scheme she'd chosen for her son's room. The border looked perfect. Once the walls were finished, they could start arranging the room to welcome the highly anticipated arrival of Matthew Wheeler Jr., which frankly, couldn't occur fast enough.

She couldn't wait to see Matt's gorgeous eyes peeking out from her child's face. But she'd have to, because she wasn't due for twenty-two very long weeks. The ultrasound the doctor performed yesterday had confirmed both gender and delivery date. The little blob on the monitor was the most beautiful thing she'd ever seen.

"Andy's still out of town," Fran remarked after Evangeline had given Carlos the okay. "Would you like to have dinner with me and Cia? The boys can fend for themselves for once."

"Thanks, that would be lovely, but I have plans with Matt. Special plans."

"Next time then." Fran smiled and turned her Southern charm on Carlos to get his help with dragging the rocker into a corner.

The ladies spent a few hours in decorating heaven until Matt strolled through the door from work, his smile for Evangeline alone.

"I'll make myself scarce." Fran winked, clearly having interpreted the definition of "special plans" in her own way, and let herself out the door.

Evangeline forgot to be embarrassed as Matt folded her into his arms.

"Hey."

"Hey, yourself." God, he smelled good, like home. Home—simple and achingly honest, and she'd never loved something so much. Roots with Matt had grown strong and solid. "Sell anything?"

"Lucas closed the deal on the Watson property. Especially sweet since I yanked it out from under Richards Group without them realizing it." His grin fluttered her stomach.

He was so happy to be working with his brother again. And she was happy she'd agreed to live in Dallas so he could. Palazzo D'Inverno waited patiently for them to return, which they planned to do after the baby was born.

"I confirmed with Lisa," Evangeline said. "She'll be here next week to start learning the new songs I wrote."

"Great. I'm looking forward to seeing her again."

Evangeline had gone to Detroit twice already, Matt firmly by her side as she worked through reconciling with her dad. Family dynamics were still new and often frustrating, but she was trying. Matt assured her that was the important thing.

"You know what today is, right?" she asked.

A guarded expression leaped onto his face. "That sounds dangerous. Is this one of those rhetorical questions that I'm already supposed to know the answer to?"

She laughed. "I'll assume that means you don't. Four months ago today, I walked into Vincenzo's palazzo, praying that no one would recognize me. I even wore a mask to ensure it, but there was this guy in the hall blocking my way. If I'd arrived one minute later, he'd have already been gone."

Matt's arms tightened, smushing her softly rounded belly into his solid body. "Sounds like fate to me."

"Absolutely. How else would I have found the one person who recognized me with a mask on?"

She tilted her head up to kiss him lightly, and lost her train of thought as he cupped her jaw to deepen the kiss.

Fate. If she still had functioning vocal cords, they'd never have met. The center of her existence had been ripped from her fingers, but its loss had made room for this man and their family. Thank goodness the fire of tragedy had refined her into someone worthy of Matt's unending devotion.

With a squeak, she broke the kiss. Reluctantly. "Let's get back to that in a sec. I got you something to commemorate our anniversary."

"You did?" He lit up. "I like your presents. The last one will be hard to top, though."

His warm hand spread over their baby, safely tucked inside her womb. "Maybe. I gave it a shot. You'll have to tell me how I did. It's in the kitchen."

She clasped his hand and led him into the kitchen he'd designed from the ground up, with dark cabinets and top-of-the-line appliances. He never minded when she invaded his domain but threatened her daily that if she hung around while he was cooking, she'd better learn something. So far, nothing had sunk in because she was too busy watching the chef's butt as he moved between the stove and the prep area.

A small bag sat on the island. Snagging it, she handed it to him. "It's an armadillo."

"A what?" One eye narrowed. "You put an armadillo in this bag?"

"Yeah. There's this thing that I need to be rescued from. So I'm calling armadillo."

With a puzzled glance at her, Matt tipped the bag up and slid the contents into his hand. She plucked the box from his palm and cracked the hinged lid to reveal a platinum band inside.

"Rescue me from being single. Will you marry me?"

His eyes went so dark with pleasure, her heart fluttered. "Nothing would make me happier. What prompted this?"

"I find myself in need of another name change." Evangeline Wheeler—another role she had no idea how to perform but couldn't wait to figure out. "This time, I'd like it to be permanent. I can't risk letting that guy from the hall get away."

And he'd promised to never again push her into a corner and demand she do something she wasn't ready for. No rules. No expectations. The decision had to be hers. She loved that about him.

"Are you sure this is what you want?" His beautiful

crystalline-blue eyes sought hers and held, hope and love shining from their depths.

She nodded. "I thought I wandered in search of fulfillment, but I was really looking for you. I love you so much. Be my armadillo."

He grinned and pulled her into his firm, safe arms. "As funny as you've been walking lately, you should be the armadillo."

"Nice. You're the one who put me in this condition. I was busy trying to soak up the Venice view, but no. You had to go and look at me like you wanted to swallow me whole." Wicked heat sizzled through his expression and arrowed straight to her girl parts. She sighed, but it came out sounding happy and content. "Yeah. Like that. I love it when you get that look."

"And I love it that we do everything out of order. I'll buy you an engagement ring tomorrow," he promised.

And then he kissed her.

* * * * *

If you loved Matthew's story,
don't miss his brother's tale,
MARRIAGE WITH BENEFITS
Available now
from Kat Cantrell and Harlequin Desire!

COMING NEXT MONTH FROM

⬥ HARLEQUIN
Desire

Available February 4, 2014

#2281 HER TEXAN TO TAME
Lone Star Legacy • by Sara Orwig
The wide-open space of the Delaney's Texas ranch is the perfect place for chef Jessica to forget her past. But when the rugged ranch boss's flirtations become serious, the heat is undeniable!

#2282 WHAT A RANCHER WANTS
Texas Cattleman's Club: The Missing Mogul
by Sarah M. Anderson
Chance McDaniel knows what he wants when he sees it, and he wants Gabriella. But while this Texas rancher is skilled at seduction, he never expects the virginal Gabriella to capture his heart.

#2283 SNOWBOUND WITH A BILLIONAIRE
Billionaires and Babies • by Jules Bennett
Movie mogul Max Ford returns home, only to get snowed-in with his ex—and her baby! This time, Max will fight for the woman he lost—even as the truth tears them apart.

#2284 BACK IN HER HUSBAND'S BED
by Andrea Laurence
Nathan and his estranged wife, poker champion Annie, agree to play the happy couple to uncover cheating at his casino. But their bluff lands her back in her husband's bed—for good this time?

#2285 JUST ONE MORE NIGHT
The Pearl House • by Fiona Brand
Riveted by Elena's transformation from charming duckling into seriously sexy swan, Aussie Nick Messena wants one night with her. But soon Nick realizes one night will never be enough....

#2286 BOUND BY A CHILD
Baby Business • by Katherine Garbera
When their best friends leave them guardians of a baby girl, business rivals Allan and Jessi call a truce. But an unexpected attraction changes the terms of this merger.

YOU CAN FIND MORE INFORMATION ON UPCOMING HARLEQUIN® TITLES, FREE EXCERPTS AND MORE AT WWW.HARLEQUIN.COM.

HDCNM0114